A COVID ODYSSEY

END IN SIGHT

A fictional COVID-19 pandemic story

Graham Elder

G.M. Elder Publishing

www.twodocswriting.com
www.grahamelder.com

Printed in Canada
Cover design by Rebecacovers

ISBN: 978-1-7388600-3-6 (ebook)
ISBN: 978-1-7388600-2-9 (pbk)

To my wife Andrea, the love of my life and soulmate.

Preface

Fair warning, if you've read the first three books in this series, this is not the book you were expecting. While it still follows the timelines of developing Covid-19 events (this time leading up to the end of September 2022), it does not continue the adventures set out in the third book. Rather, it follows Mark Spencer on a personal journey …

Prelude

There is a thought experiment:

Imagine you are dead ...

Who will come to your funeral?
Who do you wish you had settled accounts with?
What things do you wish you could've said and to whom?
What will be written on your tombstone?

For strange effects and extraordinary combinations, we must go to life itself, which is always far more daring than any effort of the imagination.

Arthur Conan Doyle

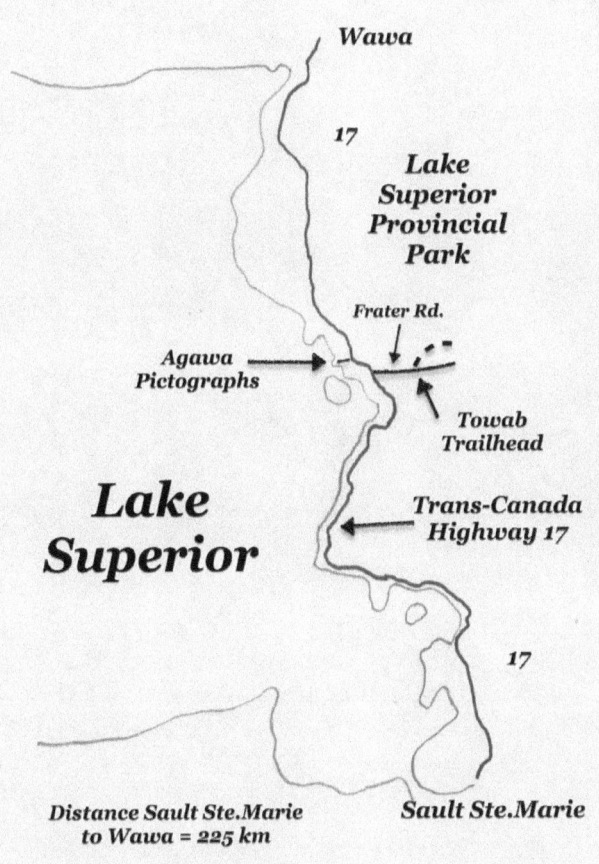

Wawa

17

**Lake
Superior
Provincial
Park**

Frater Rd.

Agawa
Pictographs

*Towab
Trailhead*

**Lake
Superior**

**Trans-Canada
Highway 17**

17

Distance Sault Ste.Marie
to Wawa = 225 km

Sault Ste.Marie

Chapter 1

Friday, September 30th, 2022

8:30 AM

I feel the bullet penetrate my skull, heavy with pressure, then darkness. It is the last thing I remember before I die.

There is a period of emptiness, of nothingness. And then awareness returns. But not really. Not like normal seeing and hearing and smelling. Not like I'm looking from one vantage point or hearing from one discrete place. It's more like I am everywhere and nowhere at once.

At first, my senses are overloaded, a kaleidoscopic spectrum of rainbows, a disorganized orchestra of sounds, an odorous whirlwind of wildflowers and trees. Slowly, each sense becomes focused, and a scene forms in my mind. I'm lying prone, still wearing my sweat-stained, light-green hiking cap, with my face pushed deep into the dirt of the Towab Trail. A day pack is hanging from my shoulders, loosely askew to the side. My arms and legs are sprawled at awkward angles to the ground, and a crimson puddle is expanding from the base of my skull.

The early morning light is breaking through the long trunks of towering maples and casting sharp, elongated shadows over my corpse. The land is flat to the horizon in all directions with no underbrush, almost like a desert, except for the trees. The trail is clearly marked with decades of packed footprints, but you could walk in any direction unimpeded, if you knew where you were going.

The sound of heavy work boots trudging on dried leaves approaches from the east, and a man dressed in green hunting camo, wearing a black mask, and carrying a scoped rifle stands over my body and looks down. He holds his rifle by the barrel with the butt end on the ground for support as he kneels. He removes a glove and places two fingers on my neck. After a moment, he bows his head and shakes it slowly from side to side.

"He's dead. I did it. I really killed him."

He stands briskly and steps back, as if he is suddenly afraid of me. He looks up at the sky, lets out a deep moan and throws his rifle to the side before falling to his knees, lifting his ski mask above his nose, and heaving his guts into a small ditch on the side of the trail. He keeps repeating, "Had to do it. Had no choice …"

When he has nothing left inside, he stands slowly, unsteadily, and wipes his sleeve across his mouth. He drops the ski mask back in place and then picks up a branch with leaves still attached. He sweeps the area around my body, removing all traces of his presence. He launches the branch, grabs his rifle, takes one last look at me, and then marches back into the woods.

It is an odd feeling. My consciousness – my being – is pulled behind him, as if I were a balloon on a long string floating overhead. I look back at my body and already I can barely recognize it as myself. I am gone. I should be sad – the death of myself – but I'm not. I feel that I'm caught up in something more important.

I trail the killer through the woods, weaving around and sometimes through the trees. The sun continues its ascent, and I can feel its warmth.

The killer pushes hard, dodging branches and curving around trunks, finally emerging into a small creek with ankle high water gurgling happily downstream. He follows the creek for some time, boots slapping the water. Is he covering his tracks, erasing any scent that a dog might follow? Does he know about such things?

He comes out of the creek, climbs an embankment, and joins an unmarked trail. He turns left and continues. Although there are no markings, and it is clear that few people venture here, there is a definite path where occasional boot prints can be seen.

His breathing is labored, and a multitude of long, desperate sighs intermittently escape his mouth. He is hunched over with shoulders sagged, the act of killing weighing heavily. There is something familiar about him. Something in his stride, in the way he holds himself.

Finally, he breaks through onto a rugged dirt road where a large Ontario Provincial Police pickup truck is parked at the side, its large front grill and roof lights clearly in keeping with its purpose. My stomach tightens. He removes his mask and shoves it deep into his jacket pocket. I'm looking at the back of his head which sports disheveled, cropped black hair two lockdown months past its need of a haircut. It looks familiar. I need to see his face. A bird takes flight from a nearby tree, and the killer turns to look for it.

That face.

I recognize him immediately.

My brother.

Chapter 2

9:15 AM

He fiddles with the radio as he comes off Frater Road and turns north on to highway 17, finally settling on a classical music station and the melodic cadence of a Bach concerto – I had no idea he likes classical music. I'm in the passenger seat, staring at the profile of his face, looking for a clue, a reason, an explanation. Something. Anything. I love my brother, and, to the best of my knowledge, he loved me. Clearly, my knowledge is lacking.

How could he?

Strangely, my emotions seem blunted, like my veins are shot through with Valium. Almost as if I'm simply an objective observer bearing witness to an ungodly event – or perhaps a godly one? Where is my hate and anger? My bloodlust for revenge? He shot me dead. My own brother killed me for no reason I'm aware of.

We had always been in each other's lives, more or less. Except when I was in Montreal studying medicine, and he was in Toronto at the Police Academy. We grew apart somewhat during this time, both of us following our respective, divergent paths. And then those paths crossed once again when we returned to Northern Ontario. I set up my practice in Sault Ste. Marie, and he ultimately became the Ontario Provincial Police (OPP) staff sergeant in Wawa, 225 kilometers to the north.

This morning, I awoke before dawn and was driving north, planning to do some locum work at the Lady Dunn Hospital emergency room and lend a hand to my sick, overworked colleagues. Although we mostly had a handle on it now, Covid-19 was still kicking our asses with waves of sickness washing over our small towns intermittently, as effectiveness of the repeated vaccines faded in the face of new variants. It wasn't so much how sick people were getting – although a lot of people still described it as the worst cold they'd ever had – but *how many* people were getting sick. It seemed everyone knew someone who was ill and taking time off from work, school, or life, hunkering down at home. And you could get it more than once with seemingly shorter and shorter intervals between sickness. Benched from society over and over again. And then there were the unfortunate souls with long-haul symptoms ….

I was enjoying an early morning hike before work, clearing my head of all the gloom and doom, when I … died? It's still too much to process.

What the hell is going on?

We drive north for an hour, and I stare at him, boring invisible daggers into the side of his head the whole while. His mood is erratic. At times shaking his head slowly from side to side, like a heavy grand-father clock pendulum, talking nonsense to himself with the whites of his eyes glowing so bright that his pupils seem to disappear. At other times, he's laughing uncontrollably with tear drops splashing over the steering wheel. My heart aches for him and, at one point, I reach out with my finger to wipe away a tear from his cheek, and then I remember:

You killed me, you bastard.

We pull off the highway at the exit for Wawa onto Mission Road. He seems more normal now, as if he's come to terms with something. He drives a half mile to an intersection, where Winston Road crosses Mission Road, eases onto the shoulder, and parks. He pulls his phone from his jacket pocket, places it on the dash, takes a deep breath and folds both arms on the steering wheel. He then cradles his forehead with his arms. I'm totally confused.

What are we doing here?

I survey the intersection we are facing and note construction in progress with a set of temporary traffic lights erected overhead and a worker standing at a control panel at its base. He seems unhappy and keeps adjusting something with his hands on the panel and then looking up to the lights. At one point he steps back and throws his work gloves at the panel.

My brother's phone alarm suddenly vibrates, accompanied by a ringtone version of Pachelbel's Canon. His head jerks and his eyes dart to the intersection. He sits bolt upright, as if his heated seat has short-circuited, and grips his steering wheel, blanching his knuckles. He looks once more at his phone, takes a deep breath, and holds it.

At the intersection, the worker who is adjusting the traffic light turns away to yell something to a fellow worker. I look up and, from our vantage point, can see the lights targeting both directions, North and West.

They are both green.

From one direction, heading west along Winston Road, a white Honda Pilot SUV approaches at high speed. From our side of the lights, heading north on Mission Road, a FedEx delivery truck whizzes by. Both see green lights and a collision appears imminent, until the FedEx truck jams its brakes, swerves just a little and screeches to a halt a few feet into the intersection with black vapours seeping from the rubber left on the pavement. The driver of the Honda Pilot seems oblivious and drives through unscathed.

The worker tending the traffic light throws his orange helmet to the pavement and begins shouting. The FedEx driver rolls down his window and yells expletives at anyone who will listen. The intersection erupts into a chaotic frenzy.

I peer sharply at the receding SUV, recognition tugging at my memory, willing myself to make out the driver's face seen through the lightly tinted windows as it speeds by. I know the driver.

It's my niece, my brother's daughter.

A loud whoosh of released, stale breath fills the air and startles me. I turn to look at my brother, and I'm shocked to find his eyes closed and a jubilant smile plastered across his face. He then begins slamming the steering wheel with both hands, shouting, "Yes. Yes. Yes!"

He quickly reaches for his phone and taps a number. A soft female voice hesitantly answers, "Hello."

"It worked. She made it. She's alive."

There is nothing but dead silence on the other end.

"I'm coming home."

He taps out and starts his truck. He pounds the steering wheel one last time as he shouts, "Fuck. I'm not crazy. It's all real. Completely real."

My brother pulls his large pick-up police cruiser onto the highway, completely disregarding traffic, eliciting a weak honk from an oncoming car. He is the law, and he should have stopped to restore peace and order. But he drives right through the intersection as bystanders look on with brows furrowed.

Chapter 3

10:18 AM

I'm now sitting in the passenger seat of my niece's SUV. I have no recollection of how this came to be; it simply is. It appears I have become the omniscient narrator able to be wherever I need to be to experience this story. *My story.* Classical music is also playing on her satellite radio, and I wonder who influenced who. I haven't seen my niece in many months, perhaps over a year. We live several hundred kilometers apart, and the only real opportunities come when there are important family gatherings, or I'm doing locum shifts in Wawa. These shifts had been mostly eliminated because of the lockdowns, as had family gatherings.

My, Rebecca, niece is a whiz kid, pure and simple. She rocketed through school skipping multiple grades and, as a result, graduated from Stanford at the tender age of 19 with a degree in microbiology. She's currently finishing her PhD program and is now 22 years old but holds herself as a woman a decade more mature. Her long straight hair, black as a moonless night, drops below her shoulder blades, and her dark complexion reflects her mother's Ojibwe heritage. Thick-lensed, black rimmed glasses frame wide, curious eyes, and she carries a knowing smile that always seems to suggest she understands something more than everyone around her.

She is humming along to the music when her phone rings, and she answers it by toggling a button on the steering wheel. I can't believe she remains completely oblivious to the accident that almost happened.

"Hello?" She says, the music automatically muting out.

"You're onto something. I mean *really* onto something big."

"Seriously? How big?"

"Like Nobel big. I thought you were crazy tackling this project for your thesis, but damn …."

I could see her chest expand, taking in a large, proud breath.

"There is one thing, though," the caller continues, "your second equation is formulated wrong. Small error. I've emailed you."

"Small error?" She cries out, both hands leaving the wheel. "Small error? The rest of my proof depends on it."

"You're close. You'll figure it out. Read my email. Maybe it will jog some neurons."

She releases a long sigh. "Alright. Thanks for the best and worst news."

She toggles the call off and then yells, "Damn. So close."

I watch her head sag just a little as both hands grip the steering wheel hard and she mutters, "I need a place to think."

She pulls onto the shoulder, checks her side-view mirror, and pulls a U-turn. She drives back to the intersection where the accident almost occurred – the temporary lights now working, and the commotion resolved – and turns right, eventually ending up on the Trans-Canada highway going south. I have no idea where she is going and, I suspect, neither does she.

Chapter 4

10:30 AM

I morph back into my brother's truck, once again sitting next to him on the passenger side just as he pulls into his driveway. His jubilation with events at the intersection seems to have evaporated during his short drive home, and his mood is sombre. He exits his vehicle and walks slowly, almost apprehensively, to the side-door of his bungalow. He opens the unlocked door and reflexively hangs his belt and sidearm on a big brass hook just inside the door. His wife doesn't allow weapons in the house, and the big brass hook is the compromise, something I had given him as a birthday gift when he joined the Wawa OPP detachment. He lumbers up a short flight of stairs to the kitchen and removes a bottle of bourbon from the cupboard above the refrigerator along with a tumbler. He collapses into a chair at the kitchen table and pours himself three thick fingers. He closes his eyes and knocks back the entire glass.

I can hear light footsteps approaching and a woman, who looks strikingly like her daughter, Rebecca, appears in the doorway. She has puffy eyes and tear streaks on both cheeks. Winona whispers, "Did you really do this, Ed? I thought you put all of it out of your head. I thought you were going to work early to catch up on paperwork. Did you really kill the man in your vision? The man is … dead?

The man? They don't know it's me.

My brother is nodding his head slowly, staring blankly at the wall across from the kitchen table. He states firmly, "And Rebecca is alive."

Winona plants herself in the chair opposite him, directly in his line of sight. Her voice is stronger now. "Damn it. Of course, she's alive. I told you. Visions are not meant to be taken literally."

There is a weird tornado of bipolar emotions swirling in the room – manic elation and depressive sadness – mixed with grief, nervousness, fear, and pity. I feel very little other than curiosity.

How is my death and my niece's life connected?

She reaches over and places her hand on top of his. "Oh, my husband, what have you done?"

He pulls his hand away abruptly and slaps the table hard. "What have I done? What I've done is saved our daughter's life."

Winona bows her head. She looks frustrated. She has spent a marriage lifetime being supportive of her husband through a lot of emotional turmoil that I was never aware of, including a rough three years when Ed was battling the bottle. She has always been there for him and always will be no matter what. No surprise, since my brother rescued her from a horribly abusive marriage that left her on death's door. She literally owes her life to my brother's love.

She looks up and sighs, "I thought we talked this through. Visions are mostly metaphorical, ideas to incorporate into your life to give you direction."

My brother's eyes are a little wild with a savage twitch to them. "Damn it, Winona, I told you, my vision wasn't like what you've described to me in the past with your visions. I didn't have a choice. The vision was relentless and wouldn't leave me alone until I committed."

"Well, that will go over well in front of a judge," Winona says sardonically. She then stands and postures a hand on each hip. "Your honor, I know I'm a cop and sworn to uphold the law, but I had to shoot and kill an innocent man because I had a mystical vision that clearly showed a future where he would drive through an intersection and kill my daughter. I hope you understand …"

"Fuck! What do you want from me? Do you think it was easy to kill a man in cold blood? Crazy, fucking spirit visions," he mumbles. He pours another three fingers and swirls the glass, staring at it.

Winona is eying his glass disapprovingly. "Careful. Don't mock what you don't understand," she warns, wavering a pointed finger at both him and his glass. "I'm not even sure what you experienced can be called a vision. It was something else."

Winona sits down and, once again, puts her hands over my brother's hands. "Are you okay?"

He looks at her. "Okay? I just shot and killed an innocent man. Holy shit! This is your mystical … stuff, and you don't even believe me. What the hell? Am I losing it?" A slow tear squeezes from the corner of his left eye.

She pauses, then gently says, "Interpreting visions can be challenging. Only you can understand what happened to you, and you did the best you could – regardless of the consequences – to save our daughter."

"So, no one can understand it but me, and even I don't understand it?"

"Did things from your vision happen as you expected?"

He releases a lengthy sigh and says, "Yes. She's alive. And everything took place exactly as the vision predicted. I just don't understand why all of this is happening."

He looks at her with doleful, pleading eyes. "Can you speak to one of your elders? Someone who knows about these things?"

"Now, it's too late. Now, we deal with the consequences. It is what it is, and I will help you every step of the way. But we must not tell anyone. Okay? No one. You must go about your business like nothing ever happened. Bury it and forget about it. Okay?"

How could he forget? He'll find out eventually that it was me, and then every time he looks at Rebecca …

He nods his head and cradles his face in his hands. The adrenaline rush is gone, and the full impact of what he's done is starting to register.

"Did you get rid of the evidence?" Winona asks.

My brother shakes his head.

"Well, you better get on that."

He closes his eyes hard, takes one more belt from his topped-up glass, sets it on the table, and then rises. He looks hard at his wife, deep into her eyes. "Yeah, I'd better get on that."

"And you'd better lay off the bourbon."

Logic surrenders to emotion, and he swipes the back of his hand across the table launching the partially filled tumbler into the wall, showering crystal fragments everywhere and leaving a blotchy brown stain on the flowery wallpaper. His drunken face looks dangerous, like a man capable of killing.

"Yeah, I'd better lay off the booze."

He goes back out the side kitchen door, pausing to eye his firearm hanging on the brass hook, his hand reflexively hovering over it, before he shakes his head and walks to his truck. He stands in front of the driver's passenger door and looks up and down the street. He opens the door and is reaching for his rifle when he hears the sound of plastic wheels rolling on crushed gravel. A voice behind him yells, "Hey, boss, good to see you up and about. We missed you yesterday. I guess you're feeling better. Any luck with the hunt?"

His blood turns to ice, his body goes rigid, and his stomach flips. He's still wearing his green camo outfit. He recognizes the voice instantly and turns to face his second-in-command and neighbor, Ryan. The sound of the rolling wheels stops. He stalls for a second, partially closing the truck door, before turning to face him.

"Yeah, all better. Really bad migraine."

"I didn't know you got migraines, boss. Sorry to hear that."

"Yeah, like I said, all better now."

"I can see that." Ryan waves a hand up and down, taking in Ed's appearance. "Looks like you got an early start today. So ... any luck?"

"Naw. Saw a bull, but too far to take the shot."

His neighbor resumes pulling his garbage bin to the curb and smiles as he yells, "Well, that's a win for the moose population, I guess." Ryan is the rare individual in town who doesn't hunt, apparently for ethical reasons. "I'm sure you'll have other opportunities. Hey ... loving this new schedule with the occasional late shifts."

"Thanks. Glad it's working out for you. Okay, gotta get cleaned up. See you at the office."

Ryan is starting back up the driveway when he suddenly turns and says, "You look a little jittery this morning, Ed. Not that it's any of my business but, besides the migraine, is everything alright? You and the missus have a spat again?"

My brother pauses for a moment before lying, "Yeah. Yeah, we're okay. Got some financial problems with the mortgage on the house. Meeting with the bank this week to sort it out."

I recall Ed does have some problems with his mortgage and a few missed payments, but that sure as hell isn't why he's jittery. Or is it? I lent him the down payment on the house two years ago as well as a few thousand more to help with payments over the past couple of months. But he doesn't even know it's me he's killed. Does he?

"Ahh, well, better financial problems than marital problems, although one can sure lead to the other, eh?"

"You sure got that right, Ryan."

"Hey, better wipe the muck off your boots before you go in the house, or the missus will tan your hide." Ryan is staring at Ed's boots. "Looks like you were in the park."

Ed looks down and notices the reddish, grey tinge of the dried mud on his boots. Everyone knows this is unique to certain parts of Lake Superior Park, where no hunting is permitted. Ed winks at Ryan. "I won't tell, if you don't."

Ryan winks back, "Roger, boss. See you at the station."

It is understood that there are perks to being on the police force and, in particular, to being the boss, as long as they aren't abused.

Ryan walks back to his house, leaving Ed to complete his "dealing-with-the-evidence" problem. He reaches into the backseat and pulls out the murder weapon – essentially a SWAT type sniper rifle. Once again, he looks up and down the street, and, this time, more closely at his neighbor's house, specifically at the side window. His attention is diverted to a moving curtain in the front window of his own house, and he sees Winona looking on. He quickly shuts the truck door and enters his detached garage.

Once inside, he places the rifle on his workbench and then expertly dismantles it. At one point, he holds a portion of the rifle up to a work light and then examines it with a magnifying glass. He removes an electric grinder from a nearby shelf, dons safety glasses, and goes to work on the serial number. When he's done, he uses the same grinder to cut the barrel in two and then places each half in a bench clamp. He uses a power drill with a long bit to drill down the center bore of the barrel, removing any markings that could be associated with the bullet that is either lodged deep in my brain, somewhere in a tree, or deep in the dirt back on the Towab Trail.

Despite the coolness of the morning, I can see droplets of sweat forming at his temples. Sporadically, he wipes them away with the backside of his work glove. If it wasn't for the sweat, I would swear I'm watching a robot at work. Precise, practiced movements, like he's done it all a million times before. I had no idea my brother knew so much about guns. But then again, he has been a cop for a long time, and he's a hunter. When his work is complete, he places the remnants of the rifle into an old army-type duffel bag along with two bricks.

He then checks the pockets of his camo gear and removes six bullets, plus the one casing from the bullet that he used to kill me. Seven has always been my brother's lucky number. He juggles the bullets and casing from one hand to the other, as if he's trying to make up his mind about what to do with them. He places the casing on an anvil, hits it with a hammer until it's flattened, and then throws it into the duffel bag. Next, he dials the combo to his gun locker, removes a box of bullets, and replaces the six remaining bullets into their respective slots. He tosses the whole box into the duffel bag.

He removes all his camo gear – jacket, pants, gloves, mask, and boots – and stuffs them into the duffel bag. He dons a flannel shirt and jeans, taken from a wall hook where they were left hanging at 5 AM this morning, and puts on a pair of sandals. He then grabs the duffel bag and steps outside and places it on the rear seat of his truck. He locks the door of his truck and garage, looks at his watch, and goes back into the house.

Chapter 5

11:00 AM

"Drink this," Winona says, setting a steaming cup of coffee in front of him at the kitchen table. "The staff sergeant can't show up for work smelling like a whisky still."

"You *are* going to work?" She asks.

"Have to act normal, right? Like nothing happened. Plus, I have to keep an eye on things, right?"

Winona is watching Ed, as if she's trying to assess the sincerity of his words and whether he is really capable of following through on them – act normal, keep an eye on things. "Well, you have an hour. Maybe you should get some sleep. Have a nap."

Ed's eyes widen and his brows spike. "Sleep? Kill a man, take care of the evidence, and then go for a nap? Are you serious? I couldn't sleep now if my life depended on it."

"Ed." She looks at him with sad eyes and softly says, "Your life *may* depend on it. You need to calm down and get it together or someone will notice something … like Ryan just did."

The air is thick with misery and there is a long, heavy pause as they both stare at each other. Finally, his wife says, "You've barely talked to me since this all started. Have your visions stopped?"

"They stopped the minute I resolved to kill an innocent man."

"And there was no other way …?"

"Every single other option I came up with to keep him from that intersection resulted in her death. If I slashed his tires in the Towab parking lot, the visions would show a vehicle giving him a lift into town and through the intersection. If I parked my truck across the intersection beforehand, for some reason I would have to move before the time came. If I tried phoning her to tell her to stay the hell away, she either wouldn't get the call, or she would ignore it. If I drove over to talk to her, for whatever reason, she wouldn't answer the door. You know how she gets when she's deep in thought, far, far away, like she's on another planet."

"Did you call her anyway?" Winona asks, her head tilted to the side.

"A dozen times since the vision began last evening. Went to voicemail repeatedly."

"You could have asked me to call?"

"Wouldn't have made a difference." He releases a long sigh and his shoulders slump.

Winona picks up her cell, goes to contacts, and dials. A voice answers immediately.

"Hello? Mom?" The white noise hum of a vehicle underway can be heard in the background.

She looks at Ed and tilts her head to the other side this time. "Hi, honey. How are you?"

"Super great and super bad, all at once. My PhD supervisor just called and told me my thesis idea has huge potential. Maybe even a Nobel prize. But there's a problem I have to figure out first. I'm just driving around right now looking for a quiet place to think. How are things at home."

"We're fine. Your dad's just getting ready for work. Why don't you come by for dinner tonight. I'll make your favorite. Maybe it will stimulate your brain a little."

"Mom, I'm super tempted, but I have to work through this glitch in my thesis, first. I may even drive to The Soo, just for the scenery."

"Well, if you think you'll be back around dinner, call me. We'll keep an extra plate."

"Okay. Thanks, Mom. Gotta go. Love to Dad."

Winona looks up from her phone at Ed and tilts her head to the side once more.

Ed slams his palms into the table nearly knocking both coffee cups over. He yells, "Of course now you can contact her. She's alive because of what I did. I was only blocked before when everything was in limbo …"

He stands from the table, a towering figure relative to his wife. "Damn you. I'm not crazy. This is your family folklore, not mine. Long ago, you convinced me visions were real."

"Ed, the power of visions is real and comes from outside of you, from the universe. What you do with it comes from within. As I said earlier, I'm not even sure what happened to you was a vision."

It's clear to me that Winona is trying desperately to reason with Ed. To make him understand that what he's done... there is no word for what he's done.

"I had no choice," he repeats for the millionth time.

"It's unfortunate you couldn't talk to the man before you –"

"Yeah, because that would have made it easier. Looking an innocent man in the eyes before I put a bullet through his brain."

"You may have reasoned with him. You may have realised there was another way. That your vision could be interpreted differently."

Ed is still standing, and he stretches himself to his full height. "Reasoned with him? Are we on the same page here? The vision was very clear on this. Talking to him would have changed nothing. Think about how that conversation would have gone. A complete stranger approaching a man on a peaceful, private morning hike:

"Hey there, stranger."

"Umm, Hi."

"Listen, I need to tell you something. I had a vision. When you're done hiking, if you head to Wawa, as you're planning to, there will be a malfunction with some temporary traffic lights set up for construction, and you're going to accidentally kill my daughter in a car accident. If you agree to not return to Wawa today at 10:18 AM, I won't kill you. Okay? Do we have a deal?"

"Fairly certain the response would have been, 'You're insane. Fuck off and leave me alone.'"

Ed slumps into his chair again, looking defeated. "Christ, maybe I *am* insane."

His wife comes around the table and places a hand on his shoulder. "Visions can be powerful. You felt you had no choice."

"Right, I had no choice," he agrees. Now his elbows are on the table with his hands cradling his chin. Tears are streaming down his cheeks. "In twenty years of law enforcement, I've never taken a life. I've only had to pull my weapon from its holster three times."

He turns his head to stare down the short flight of stairs at his gun hanging on the hook, the purest and most distilled representation of his position of authority as a police officer.

He never sees it coming. His wife's hand roundhouses a slap across his face so hard it explodes like a gunshot.

"What the –"

She's staring at him with wide eyes and pursed lips, her whole body shaking. "Pull it together, Ed. Your life depends on it. Plus, I don't need to lose another husband. If you can't nap, go upstairs, and have a shower. I'll make you breakfast. Then you're going to deal with the evidence, go to the station, and act like it's a very normal day."

Winona could be an absolute firecracker when she needed to be. It's how she sobered Ed up, and how she's kept him dry all these years. Until now.

Ed is rubbing his face where a small, red handprint is starting to glow. He pulls a sleeve across his eyes and croaks, "Yes, Ma'am."

Chapter 6

11:45 AM

A familiar countryside drifts by my brother's truck window, like a slideshow at a celebration of life funeral, memories long forgotten taunting me: The church where my brother married, with its newish solar panels on its peaked roof in the shape of a cross; the 28-foot-high Wawa Canada Goose, where I first kissed my wife under a near full moon – my wife, the widow.

For the first time since my death, my thoughts extend more fully to all those connected to me: my wife, Sarah, a pharmacist at my hospital; my daughter, June, now fourteen months old and showing no long-term sequelae from her Covid-19 battle ten months earlier; my frail mother, Frances, who still lives alone in England. What will they do without me? And what about my colleagues and friends, like Rick and Hitchhiker? Will they miss me? How long before my face becomes a fuzzy picture in their minds, that guy they knew once upon a time?

It crushes me to think I will never create new memories, and what memories I have will soon disappear with the ashes of my corporal body. At that moment, I suddenly realize that this ephemeral journey I am on has an unknown purpose and an end in sight. I'm not fully dead yet, but I soon would be. I glance up at the mid-day sun and instinctively know it is the last time I will follow its arc through the sky. My afterlife-time is finite. This momentary reprieve from death is a gift with an expiry date.

We turn off the highway onto Michipicoten road where asphalt becomes gravel and potholes push the truck around like a little Hot Wheel toy. We pull into Buck's Marina, and Ed grabs his duffel bag full of evidence, walks across the dock, and boards the detachment's police boat. He throws the duffel bag onto the deck and then fires up the outboard engines. I'm sitting in the co-pilot's chair and watch him release the lines and then take the helm. We are apparently going out to sea, onto Lake Superior.

A late morning mist has settled on the Michipicoten River. The mist is buffeted and swirled by a westerly wind, plastering the front windows and obscuring visibility. He switches on the windshield wipers, and they squeal like pigs pushed to the slaughter. He stiffens visibly at the sound and quickly turns them off. He sticks his head out the side window and navigates through the narrow channel, negotiating his way between red and green markers, something he's done since he was a child and could almost do blindfolded. For reasons unclear to me, I am savoring this strange, macabre *Hearts of Darkness* journey, watching the salmon clear the water like high jumpers and the Bald Eagles circle overhead until they acquire their targets and swoop in for the kill, sometimes picking the salmon out of the air, midjump. There is so much life – and death – on these waters.

We emerge from the river and into turbulent waters where the flow of the Michipicoten River fights to join Lake Superior. Our boat corkscrews and bobs around eddies and troughs before finally passing the entrance marker into the long, heavy swells of the largest freshwater lake in the world. My brother guns the engines, and we head west, out to open water. We pass a solar powered metal scaffolding lighthouse that marks the northern part of Michipicoten Bay. It is surrounded by dilapidated buildings once home to the lighthouse keeper. He turns on the radio and, ironically, Gordon Lightfoot is singing that part from *The Wreck of the Edmond Fitzgerald* about the lake never giving up her dead. The soaring electric guitar makes me think of a distraught mermaid or a whale and sends shivers up my non-existent spine.

We push on until we are several miles out to sea and the horizon disappears. Large waves bounce the boat around as if the skipper needs a reminder of how insignificant he is in the scheme of three quadrillion gallons of water. My brother needs no reminder and neither do I. He and I have survived many adventures on Gitchee Gumee. Often, just barely. Surviving only because we helped each other beat the odds.

My brother throttles to neutral, allowing the boat to drift, letting the waters of Superior take control. He is crying again as he lifts the duffel bag, pauses for a moment, and then drops it over the side. He peers over the gunnel and watches the bricks inside the bag drag his murder weapon into the depths, lost forever among the many dead souls that came before me.

Chapter 7

1:00 PM

Ed struts into the police station like he owns the place with authoritarian nods to some underlings and curt hellos to others. It's difficult to assess the reactions of the half-dozen or so employees here this afternoon because the majority are wearing masks.

Can they see it's all an act?

I doubt it. I would guess that for them this is fairly ordinary behavior. Ed generally likes to put on a good show of confidence, and, given how much his staff respect him, this is clearly what they expect.

Normally, there would be a dozen or more employees at this police station: clerks, administrators, detectives, and officers. Now, like hospitals and public organizations everywhere, staff shortages from illness rule the day. It's not *if* someone will call in sick on a given day but how many. And whether or not there will be enough left to get the job done. You would think, under these circumstances, policy or not, everyone would be wearing a mask. But I get it. Once upon a time, for me, masks were simply a means of protection, a defensive tool permitting me to do my job. Now, they have become a trigger. A reminder of everyday life continuously colliding with the pandemic era of the last three years. A reminder of all the insane adventures – Florida, Montreal, England, Providencia, Nicaragua – I've survived to save loved ones on the brink of death from Covid-19.

With the exception of hospitals and nursing homes, we are now in a period of optional masking based on personal preference. If you are sick, you are wearing a mask to protect others. If you are well, you are wearing a mask to protect yourself from getting sick. Since it's a preference, at least people are generally wearing appropriate medically approved masks, as opposed to the balaclavas or neck gaiters of the early days.

Ed beelines for his office, closing the door loudly so that everyone can hear he is not to be disturbed. A full breakfast with a side order of TLC from his wife has bolstered his spirits and his confidence considerably. Not to mention getting rid of the incriminating evidence. I can see through the façade, though: The way he doesn't look anyone in the eye, the way he keeps his eyes glued to the floor, the slight tremor to his gun hand. He owns nothing of this place right now.

I remain as lost and confused as ever. All I really understand is that my death is somehow related to my niece's life, at least on some magical plane that my scientific mind comes up desperately short of explaining. That, and the fact my brother apparently has no idea who he has killed, that he has murdered his own flesh and blood.

Winona has experienced visions throughout her life; was she privileged to some kind of "vision" as well? Did she secretly push him to do the deed? Did Winona know I was the target? Does she really believe Ed had some kind of vision? It didn't seem so. She and I have always gotten along, but if it came down to a choice between her daughter and her brother-in-law, there really would be no choice. And I couldn't blame her for that.

I could, however, blame this whole absurdity on mystical, magical thinking. Or is this more appropriately diagnosed as some sort of psychosis. Maybe a folie à deux? Or folie à trois since I seem to be a part of this bizarre delusion. My paranoia is running wild. I can feel my anger boiling to the surface, and then, it's as if someone has taken the lid off, releasing the steam. A bolus of tranquilizer coursing through my blood. I want so desperately to be angry, to lash out. I will never see my wife again, my baby girl, or my mum. My friends. Maybe I would be visiting my father. We still have much to say to each other. Much that had not been said before he died. And maybe ... Rufus?

Why am I here?

My brother closes the door to his office, sits down at his desk and busies himself. I can see he is going through the motions, slumped over, accomplishing very little. He looks up at a ship's wheel clock on the wall frequently. Is he expecting something? Or is he just anxious for the day to end? A knock on the door straightens his spine as if iron girders have been inserted.

"Come."

The door cracks open and an anxious face peers through. "Boss."

"Ryan." Ed waves him in and says, "What's up?"

He steps through the door and stands in front of Ed's desk. "We got something bad. A body. On the Towab Trail about three kilometers from the trail head. Hiker came across it about twenty minutes ago and called it in. Says it's gruesome, blood everywhere. He was barely getting his words out between retching."

If Ryan notices the color drain from my brother's face, he doesn't show it. I can only imagine what's going through my brother's mind. *Oh! No worries. I already know all about it. That's the guy I shot in the head with my rifle this morning before breakfast.*

"Bear attack?"

I have to give him credit. He's warming up to the show.

"Probably. Or maybe an angry moose."

"So, no ID?"

Ryan shakes his head. "Not so far."

Ed makes a show of closing a file. "Did you send someone?"

"Not yet. Listen. There's something else. The retching didn't stop the witness from snapping a shot with his phone and posting it."

"You're shitting me?"

"I'm not. Facebook, Instagram, Twitter, even freaking TikTok. By now it probably has a million

34

views. The press will be knocking on our door very shortly."

Ed stands from his desk. His right leg buckles imperceptibly. "We need to get over there."

"What about the press?"

"Set up a blockade on Frater Road at the entrance off the highway. No press. Tell them we'll release a statement when we know more."

Chapter 8

2:10 PM

I'm once again riding shotgun in Ed's patrol vehicle. Both of his hands remain firmly on the wheel in the old textbook 2 and 10 o'clock positions for the entire ride. He never once edges above the 90 km/hr speed limit. His seat belt is on – something he typically feels is optional. It's as if he's trying to be the model citizen to make up for his recent transgression of first degree murder. I'm sure Ryan, who's following behind, is scratching his head asking himself why Ed is driving so slowly to a potential crime scene.

Is it, perhaps, that it's the last place on earth Ed wants to be?

Ryan isn't as dumb as Ed thinks he is. He's going to notice Ed's unusual behavior and maybe, eventually, figure things out. I'm not entirely optimistic, though. With Ed's position of power as the staff sergeant, there would have to be some fairly flagrant evidence to allow Ryan to jump the hurdle and even begin to entertain the possibility that his long time boss, neighbor, and friend could do something so heinously out of character.

At this point, I still can't believe Ed has killed me based on a vision. A magical vision.

Really?

He has no psychiatric history that I'm aware of. The convoluted story of saving his daughter seems far-fetched. I've worked my mind numb trying to make sense of it all with no success, and, despite my scientifically fascinating gossamer existence, I'm actually getting a little bored and weary. That is, until a convoy of trucks passes us in the opposite direction going north, each truck plastered with large Canadian flags, and various versions of "Mandate Freedom" painted across bumpers, front grills, wind deflectors, and the sides and back of the semi-trailer. When they see our "convoy" of two police cruisers, they honk their horns furiously. It's not clear to me what these dozen or so trucks are doing or where they're going, but their passion and dedication appears unfaltering.

The Freedom Convoy protest began in January of this year, marked by hundreds – thousands? – of truckers and their rigs from all across the nation ultimately invading the downtown core of Ottawa, the nation's capital, on January 29th, where thousands of pedestrians joined them. While initially protesting Covid-19 vaccines, it later evolved into a protest of all mandates associated with Covid. Strangely, I recalled data showing that 85% of truckers nationwide were already vaccinated by January. In my mind, it was one of those instances of the few stirring up the pot for the many. Prime Minister Trudeau ultimately invoked the Emergencies Act, but it was months before order was restored. For a moment, I wonder why, eight months later with almost all Covid related mandates now repealed – QR codes no longer needed, travel restrictions lifted including the ArriveCAN app requirements effective October 1st – these truckers are still protesting. And then I realize I just don't care. It seems so inconsequential in the scheme of my non-life. In fact, almost every sensationalized Covid news-related thing I can think of seems to pale in the face of my predicament. Protests are for those who care about the future. I have no future, and all I care about are those I love. The ones I'm leaving behind. The ones I will never see again. I can feel myself taking that spiralling path of misery again. I'm quite certain it isn't normal to be able to think about your death and your loved ones after you are dead. My psyche clearly isn't equipped to handle thoughts of my own non-existence.

We finally turn off the Trans-Canada Highway onto Frater Road and are met by two police officers standing in front of their squad cars, blocking the entrance. Frater Road is an hour from Wawa and roughly two hours from Sault Ste. Marie. It would be some time still before reporters, journalists, and the "curious" arrive.

Ed nods to one of the officers who then ducks into his cruiser and backs up, leaving a small opening for our vehicle and Ryan's, who is right behind us. Ed seems miffed. He's scowling at the officer and muttering under his breath, "What? Couldn't back up a little further to give us more room? You morons are gonna be working a lot of nights." He inches the squad car through and then peels out, spitting small rocks into the air in the direction of the squad cars.

We drive the winding Frater Road, swerving around potholes and dodging low hanging branches and fallen trees, finally arriving at the entrance to the Towab Trailhead where we find one squad car, a Jeep Wrangler, and a burgundy Highlander parked. The focus of attention is clearly the Highlander.

My Highlander.

Ed and Ryan exit their vehicles at the same time. Ryan is in full professional mode – standing tall, chest out, shades in place, hand hovering around his weapon, stepping hard – and Ed is trying to be, but failing miserably. His shoulders are slack, each foot is dredging a line in the dirt road with each step. His head is sagging forward, and his pistol hand is playing awkwardly with the lining of his pocket. He appears more rookie cop than staff sergeant. He glances at Ryan, and this seems to remind him of his rank and title, what his role is here – a different role than that of the killer returning to the crime scene. He subtly shakes his head and eventually mirrors his right-hand man.

He whispers, "You take the lead on this one, Ryan. Good training."

Ryan nods to Ed and then focuses on the other cop, who is standing next to a man in his early thirties dressed in full hiking attire. "This is the witness?" he asks.

"Yes," the officer answers. "Matt Gredecki, from The Soo. He drove up late this morning and was planning an overnighter to the falls when he came across the victim."

"Listen," the officer continues, notes of anxiety creeping into his voice, "there's something you need to know. Something Matt forgot to mention when he called in."

Ryan waves the officer off. "S'okay. Let's just get it straight from him."

The officer shrugs his shoulders and steps away. Ryan and Ed turn to face Matt.

Matt seems lost in some weird trance, staring at his backpack on the ground. Eventually, he looks up and makes eye contact with Ed and Ryan. He's clean shaven and deathly pale with bloodshot eyes. He looks terribly unwell and is propped against the hood of his Wrangler, as if he might fall over without the support. No one extends hands in greeting, formalities long curtailed by the pandemic, although there is a general nod of heads. Everyone is staring at Matt, waiting for him to say something. He doesn't.

"Mr. Gredecki," Ryan begins. "You found the body?"

Matt inhales a deep breath and says, "About an hour and a half ago." He launches into his story. His voice shivers and reluctantly splutters out the words between sighs as he describes how he was off for an overnight backpacking trip and was hiking along merrily when he came across a body sprawled face first in the dirt, lying in a pool of blood. "At first, from a distance, I thought it was someone who had just fallen and injured themselves, or maybe had some heart issues and passed out. I'd seen the SUV when I arrived." He points to my Highlander in emphasis. "When I saw the blood, though, I knew it was something … else."

His head drops now, and he clutches his stomach, as if he's holding back something more than his memories.

Ryan continues, "Did you hear anything? Animal sounds, maybe?"

"Animal sounds?" Matt stiffens and his eyes turn to white saucers. "Man, this was no animal. This guy was shot in the head. I got right up close. I had to check to see if he was alive, right? Do my Good Samaritan thing, right? The side of his head was completely blown off. It was like out of a movie."

For the first time, Ryan looks unsure of himself. His eyes blink repeatedly, like he can't believe what he just heard.

"What do you mean, shot?" he fires back. Both Ryan and Ed have seen the photo circulating online; however, it's from a distance and all you can see is me lying in a pool of blood. My open cranium is not visible for the world to see, thank goodness.

"You didn't report that when you called in," Ryan continues. "You just said there was blood. From the photo we assumed it was an animal attack."

"No way, man. This was no animal. Sorry, I was freaked out when I called. I guess I thought I said he was shot, but maybe I didn't. The reception was lousy, also … I dunno."

Ed places a calming hand on Ryan's shoulder and asks Matt, "Did you hear anything? A gunshot, maybe?"

Ed wants to know if Matt was anywhere in the area when he shot me. Based on the timing he shouldn't have been, but he wants to make sure. There can't be any witnesses.

"No, nothing. There was no wind this morning, and it was very quiet. I would have heard that."

I can see the gears spinning in Ed's head.

"How much of a head start do you think the victim had on you?" He asks abruptly, somewhat accusingly.

Matt straightens instantly and stares quizzically at Ed.

"Sorry," – Ryan has regained his composure and takes over, glancing at Ed and raising an eyebrow – "my boss is just wondering how far along the trail the victim is. So that we can get an idea as to the timing."

"Right. Sorry, I'm a little off right now. I know you're just doing your job. Yeah, he looked pretty fit with all the right gear. I have no idea how long he was … down for, but, like I told this other officer, I'm guessing he was about 45 minutes into his hike before …."

Matt's head hangs loosely again as he stares at his backpack.

"And you didn't see anything suspicious or out of the ordinary on your hike or in the parking lot. Other cars?"

"No, nothing. I was completely alone. It was fucking scary, let me tell you. Once I realized the guy had been shot, I lost it for a while. I took a pic with my phone in case no one believed me and then ducked to the ground and started commando crawling into the woods next to the trail. I mean, what if it was a psycho picking off hikers randomly …?"

Ed interrupts at this point, clearly annoyed, "And you sent the pic onto social media?"

"No," Matt corrects, "just my girlfriend. I was holed up in a ditch but barely had one bar on my phone. Enough for a text, but I wasn't sure the pic would get through. I thought I was gonna die. I needed someone to know what was going on, so I sent it to her and … I guess it finally got through … and I guess she sent it to her friends … who sent it to their friends."

"You know, it's gone viral," Ed mutters, shaking his head disapprovingly.

"I'm sorry. That wasn't my intention. I was just so freaked out."

"After that?" Ryan asks.

"I crawled away from the trail through the underbrush for a bit, until I had better reception, and called 911. Then I just sat there for a while listening. I could barely hear anything over the sound of my heartbeat, but, eventually, I could tell there was no one around, and I figured if someone was watching the body waiting for another victim to show, he would have taken a shot at me already. I stayed off the trail and made my way back through the woods to the parking lot. I've been waiting for you guys to get here ever since."

I recognize Matt. He had been my patient once upon a time. I look to the back of his left wrist and see the faded markings of a laceration I had repaired in the ER. As a fellow backpacker and human being, I'm feeling deep sorrow for him and can only imagine how terrifying it must have been for him to come across my freshly killed corpse. One minute, he's enjoying the fresh air of a new adventure, and the next, he's embroiled in a murder mystery. One minute, he's running a steady elevated heartbeat building his cardio, the next, his heartrate has spiked so high he's almost in V-tach. I look at Ed and think, *look upon the ripple effect of what you've done to me.*

"Alright. If you think of anything else that can help us, like something you heard or saw, call me directly." Ryan hands Matt his card and then looks at Ed. "Anything else?"

"No." Ed is looking everywhere but directly at Matt. "You're free to go. Will you be heading back to The Soo?"

"Hell, yes." Matt is now holding both hands up in front of him towards the trailhead, like he's protecting himself with an invisible wall. "I need to get as far away from here as I can. I'll be lucky if I ever have the nerve to hike again."

"Well," Ed says, without a trace of empathy, "be sure to give us a call if you think of anything."

Ryan and Ed back away while Matt picks up his gear and throws it quickly into the back of his jeep. He then opens his door and is about to get in when he just freezes, standing there rigid with his eyes clenched shut. What color he had left in his face has all but drained. Both Ed and Ryan are staring at him, waiting. He suddenly spins and runs to the edge of the parking lot behind his jeep, bent over, dry heaving through a waterfall of tears. Ryan jogs over to offer help, but Matt puts up his hand, as if to say, "Just leave me alone."

After a few minutes, Matt returns to his jeep, this time looking more determined. He gets in, starts it up with a loud "Vroom," and then accelerates out of the parking lot, leaving a small cloud of dreary dust in his wake and the gas fumes from a muffler on its last legs.

Ryan turns to Ed. "Poor guy. He's going to be traumatized for life."

Ed is stone-faced and unreadable.

Ryan looks to the other cop, who is standing by his patrol car, and yells, "How long before the ATVs get here?"

"Over an hour," he responds.

"I guess we're going hiking," Ryan states. "You up to it, boss?"

"Not much choice. We have to cordon off the area before anybody disturbs it. Think there's a chance there's anyone coming back from the falls that might stumble across it?"

"I doubt it," Ryan replies, scanning the parking lot. "No other vehicles here but the victim's."

Ed is no doubt reflecting there are other places to park your truck to get on the trails than here in the parking lot, but he wisely chooses to keep this thought to himself. No point in planting ideas.

"Although, I suppose," Ryan reflects, looking towards the parking lot exit where the dust is just settling, "someone could be parked further up or down Frater Road. Hell, if I was the shooter, that's probably what I would do."

"Good thinking, Ryan," Ed says, swallowing hard. "Let's send someone to check on it."

Ryan steps away to use his radio while Ed sits on the open tailgate of his truck and changes out his uniform boots for his hiking shoes.

When Ryan returns, Ed asks him, "Not changing out your boots?"

"Naw, I'm good. I see you finally got those fancy new hiking shoes you ordered, with the better heel support."

"Yup. It took four months. Damn global supply chain excuse again. It's like Covid wrapped its dirty paws around everything there is in our lives."

"You got that right, boss. Ready?"

Ed stands up slowly pushing into each shoe, testing them. He sighs and then says, "Yeah. Let's get this over with."

Ryan shoulders a backpack that contains all their crime scene investigative equipment and leads the way.

Chapter 9

2:30 PM

It's late afternoon now, and the trail is dry and crisp to walk on. Twigs snap as they stomp along at a brisk pace. Before long they both remove their jackets revealing sweat streaks down their backs. They march in silence, lost in their own thoughts. I can only imagine what's going through Ed's mind as he gets closer to the crime scene. He's holding his jacket over his shoulder with his left hand while his right continuously massages the base of his neck, as if he has a nasty, guilty headache. A part of me is looking forward to seeing the look on his face when he sees his only brother lying in a pool of blood. A pool of blood that he is the author of.

Before long, they descend a lengthy downward slope that passes through a deep ravine with sloped walls rising high at an angle that would be impossible to climb without appropriate gear.

"Y'know, Ed. It's been a few years since I hiked this trail, but every time I go through this part, the ravine, I think one of two things. If a really heavy rain ever came on and you were caught here, there'd be no way to get out besides swimming for your life. Scares the crap out of me."

"And the other thing?" Ed asks.

"This would be a perfect killing zone. Someone sitting up there with a rifle could pick off anyone down here like fish in a bowl."

"Geez, Ryan. I thought hiking was supposed to be a pleasant thing that quieted the mind and put you back in touch with nature?"

"Sometimes. Sure as hell isn't right now. I can picture the shooter up there following us through his rifle scope. I can appreciate why Matt was so freaked out. If the guy really was shot, I wonder why it didn't take place here."

Without thinking, Ed says, "Well, I guess the killer would need to confirm his kill, which would mean getting down into the ravine and then somehow getting out. All without leaving a trace."

They're walking single file and Ryan stops for a moment to turn and look at Ed. "Damn, Ed. That's smart. Thinking like the killer. I guess that's why you're the boss."

For just a second, Ed makes direct eye contact with Ryan and flashes a confident grin.

Some part of him, the hunter, or the cop, is proud that he has accomplished his mission flawlessly. That he has killed me without any hiccups. He's certain that he's left no trace at the crime scene, and his weapon was efficiently disposed of and will never be found.

Winona will never talk. He's getting away with my murder. The only thing that can trip him up is a guilty conscience. Does he have a guilty conscience? There are subtle cracks in his façade.

His shoulders slouch somewhat, and his chest seems to deflate a little. I can see him trying to fall back into his role of the confident but easy-going staff sergeant letting his second-in-command take charge, but a shadow of guilt now follows him that he's impossibly trying to distance himself from.

As they exit the ravine at the bottom of the slope, Ryan suddenly stops short and points. "There."

Ed looks over Ryan's shoulder and acknowledges that, far in the distance, he, too, can make out a form lying on the trail. The sun is now high in the sky and, strangely, through a gap in the tall trees beams what almost seems like a spotlight on my body. As if mother nature is saying, "Here's what you're looking for."

Ryan's right hand immediately goes to his holstered pistol, but Ed confidently grabs his arm and says, "Trust me. The shooter's long gone." Just one more in a web of lies he is spinning today.

"Yeah, I know you're right." Ryan's hand moves away from his pistol, and he advances slowly, constantly scanning the forest from side to side, as if the shooter might pop out from behind a tree at any moment. A thick bead of perspiration trickles from Ryan's forehead, onto his cheek, and then rolls over a bounding carotid artery in his neck. His fear is palpable, and, despite Ed's reassurance, his hand continues to flutter around his holster.

When they get to within ten feet, Ryan drops his backpack and then rummages through it, pulling out a camera. He begins snapping photos of the crime scene from every angle, slowly working his way 360 degrees around the body. When he arrives at an angle where he can see what's left of my head, he pauses, drops to one knee, and says, "Damn. This guy really was shot." Murder is exceptionally rare in these parts and, despite being on the force for over ten years, this is Ryan's first murder crime scene.

"You okay, Ryan?" Ed asks.

I'm impressed by Ed's composure. How well he's holding it together. The concerned, wisely captain of his ship.

"Yeah, I'm fine. It's pretty gruesome, though."

While Ryan is taking photos, Ed strings yellow crime scene tape around the perimeter from tree to tree, following protocol.

Ryan puts his camera down and takes a long swig from his canteen. With water still dribbling from the corner of his mouth, he inhales deeply and says, "Okay, I'm going to look for some ID."

He squats in front of my body, deftly avoiding the pool of blood that is now congealed with a waxy, crimson appearance. He then begins searching through the various pockets of my orange hiking jacket, finally reaching under, and pulling my wallet from a breast pocket. He stands and flips through it, eventually finding my driver's license. He stares at it for a moment, and then a stunned, pale look comes over his face. He starts shaking his head from side to side. "No, no, it's not possible."

Ed, who is looking on from a few feet away, steps forward, and, as if on cue, says, "What's not possible?"

"Ed. Stay there. Don't come any closer."

"What? Why?"

You're about to find out why, brother of mine.

"I need to check something." Ryan kneels down again and, with some effort, turns my body into a supine position with my face up. A little wave of blood laps outwards from under the congealed surface, splashing onto his boots.

When I see my ashen, blood drained face with eyes wide open and pupils fixed, a desperate, otherworldly terror comes over me.

You're not supposed to see yourself dead.

This is something I'm quite sure of. Your psyche is not equipped to handle such an impossible thing. My sight suddenly disappears for a moment, and everything goes dark. I worry that I'm really and completely dead this time, that this strange, unearthly ride is over. And then a warm feeling comes over me, like another bolus of tranquilizer has flooded my body, and I'm able to see again, the feelings of terror abated with a detached calmness overriding everything else.

I float in place, a frustrated witness to unfolding events, unable to participate.

"Christ, Ed." Ryan whispers, "It's your brother."

Chapter 10

3:10 PM

Ed is standing a few feet away now and staring directly at my face. While the entrance wound is a clean hole at the base of my skull, the exit wound has torn half my face and head away, leaving jagged edges of bone glinting in the sun and my chin, mouth, and nose in complete disarray, like a grotesque zombie-Picasso painting. Still, I'm sure he recognizes me.

There is no acting anymore as Ed takes in a complete look of his handiwork. Not only has he taken a life, but he now knows that life belonged to his only brother. While he was holding it together up until now, as if he were playing a lead role in a dramatic play, this new knowledge releases a trapdoor under his feet that leaves him flailing. He drops to both knees, and then lunges for the edge of the trail, familiar territory from this morning, where he heaves his guts once again. Even in my ghostly form, I can feel his tortured pain.

Ryan has been doing surprisingly well until this point. However, watching his boss collapse is too much for him. He buries his head in bushes on the opposite side of the trail and follows suit.

When the retching has settled on either side of the trail, both men sit with their backs against a tree and look across to one another, locking wet, mournful eyes. Ryan is the first to speak. "Ed, I'm so sorry. So, so sorry. I can't believe it's your –"

Ryan tilts his head back and looks to the sky, as if he's searching for some heavenly explanation.

"Of all the shitty luck," he continues. "To be killed by some random, nut-job sniper. Especially since I know he was coming up here to help out in the ER with everyone off sick, trying to give our guys a break. Trying to do some good in this crappy, pandemic world." He leans forward now and buries his head in his hands, releasing a low, guttural moan.

Ed remains speechless with a blank look on his soggy face, a broken man. Part of me is elated that some preliminary deliverance of justice has been served, and I hope he feels as horrible as he looks. Another part of me, though, is still digging at the motive behind everything. Was there some logical reason I simply can't understand that explains why he did what he did? Could there ever be a logical reason to do such a thing? Did some supernatural vision really convince him to kill me to save his daughter? Has my brother lost his mind? I can't completely write him off until I know the answers to these questions.

For a fleeting moment, he seems to be looking up at me, and I want to believe he's sorry. But if there is sorrow in those eyes, it is quickly replaced by a gleam

I can only describe as calculated. Within the thump of a heartbeat, he seems to have changed. He's back on his path, now, and there is no room for apologies or guilt – only survival. Finding out that I was his victim is, apparently, merely a small bump in the road on his way down below.

He rocks forward on to his knees, as if in a praying position, looks to the sky and lets out a loud, sorrowful wail. Ryan immediately stands, walks around my body to kneel next to Ed, and places a hand on his upper arm.

"We'll get the bastard who did this, Ed. Don't you worry. If it's the last thing we do."

My brother can be a very pragmatic man, a useful quality in a police officer and one that very quickly pushed him to the head of his department. He suddenly seems to have realized that there can be no better strategy for him than to play up his role as victim. This makes me all the angrier. I drift over to him and lash out with a slap across his face, like the one Winona delivered. My hand simply ghosts through him, though. I am only here to observe. I have no part to play anymore in this tragedy.

Ryan half whispers, "Ed, you stay put. I'm going to radio this in and see how far out the forensics team is."

He digs the radio out of his backpack and walks a half-dozen yards down the trail. The radio squawks, and he begins relaying the info.

Ed, his faculties now completely online, starts looking around the crime scene. He seems to have come to grips with everything. He isn't a religious man, and neither am I, but if he was, I imagine he would be wondering what horrible tortures are awaiting his soul at the fiery gates.

He spots something in the bushes at the edge of the trail six feet away and crawls over from his sitting position. He pauses, and then begins retching again. He isn't really, though. This time it's all for show, fake retching. He has discovered some residual leftovers from earlier this morning that he hadn't covered with sand and needs to explain it away. At one point, he peeks over at Ryan to make sure he's catching his performance. He's lucky. I'm not sure if a killer can be identified by the contents of his stomach, but now he has all the bases covered. I wonder what other clues he's left behind, and I'm sure he's wondering this also. Maybe he's not as perfect a killer as he thought he was.

"They're making good time, Ed. The team should be here in ten minutes or so."

Ed stands, holding on to a young maple at the trail side for support. His voice is hoarse as he says, "Thanks, Ryan."

"You, okay?"

"No. No, I'm not okay. But I think I can hold it together. At least for now."

"Alright. We'll get a ride back on an ATV and then get you home."

Ryan hesitates a moment before he asks, "Do you want me to phone Sarah?"

Ed looks blankly at Ryan. I assume he hasn't quite thought through the cascade of events that will follow now that he knows who he's killed. Someone must inform my wife, Sarah, that I'm dead. And some day, she will have to tell my daughter, June, exactly how her father died. A little more involved than a wartime *Dear John* letter.

My thoughts turn more deeply to June. My beautiful baby girl who was born and raised during the pandemic and knows nothing but a world permanently scarred with despair and fear. She has survived so much and deserves everything good the world can offer her. A world with two parents who love her and would do anything for her. Thanks to my brother, her future is shattered.

Ed recovers quickly. "Thanks for the offer, Ryan, but I'll take care of it. She needs to hear it from me first."

"Okay. Please pass on my condolences and tell her we're going to do everything we can to find the killer. Everything."

Poor Sarah. If Ryan makes good on his word, not only will Sarah have lost her husband but also her brother-in-law. Although, I can't bear the thought of Ed consoling my wife, playing with my baby girl. It turns my stomach.

"Ryan, I don't think I'm going to be much help with this investigation."

"Of course, boss. No problem. Why don't you hike over to Burnt Rock Pool and sit by the water for a bit. It's only ten minutes from here. I'll come and get you."

"No, that's okay. I want to be nearby in case you need any help. I'll just sit down under this tree over here." The tree is approximately a dozen steps from the crime scene. Far enough that he can escape the visuals of my corpse, but close enough to keep an eye on things.

"Sure. Listen. I'm going to do a perimeter search while we wait for the team to get here."

Ryan then starts walking concentric, enlarging circles around the crime scene, his eyes glued to the ground. I can hear him sloshing in the mud at one point. I'm doubtful Ryan will find anything; despite the error with the leftover puke, my brother is too good at his craft, both as a police officer and as a hunter.

Before long, I hear the whining engines of two ATVs approaching. They stop just short of the yellow tape, and Ryan meets them immediately, bringing them up to speed. They unpack their gear and then Ryan beckons Ed to join him as he commandeers one of the ATVs. The newcomers are aware at this point of the identity of the victim and are quick to offer Ed their sympathies.

With Ryan steering and Ed sitting behind, they make the return trip in under fifteen minutes. The blur of trees on either side gives me the impression I'm riding through a tunnel, but not the fun kind that you find at a carnival, which reminds me once again of something I will never see or do again now that my life is coming to an end. Dying is really turning out to be an emotional bitch.

Chapter 11

3:40 PM

Ryan parks the ATV, leaving it running, and then checks in with the other police officer staked out in the parking lot. Ed walks slowly to his truck, his glazed-over eyes staring dully at the ground. Ryan speaks with the officer for a few minutes before returning to see Ed.

"Ed, they just found a truck parked on a rough sideroad off Frater about a kilometer from here towards the highway. The entrance is marked Sewage Lagoon. Must be some kind of sewage treatment area. It's not on any maps. They were able to follow footprints into the woods. Apparently, there's some kind of unmarked trail that's used by the locals. We still don't know where it goes, but it's possible that it hooks into the Towab."

Ed looks up, and I can see a momentary spark of concern in his eyes. Ed knows the trail, of course. It was the one he used to ambush me.

"I've never heard of any trail that connects with the Towab," he replies. "It's possible, though. Did you send someone to follow it?"

"Word has gotten out about the killing, Ed. We've got some off-duty personnel coming to give us a hand. Even the sick ones. Everyone knows it's your brother, and they want to help. Phil was already on his way to The Soo and is only ten minutes away. He has a radio and will follow the trail."

It's hard to tell from the look on Ed's face if he considers the offers of extra help more of a heartwarming testimonial to his leadership or rather another dark step into the nightmare with a noose slowly closing around his neck.

"Also," Ryan continues, "they found another vehicle parked further up the road. It's possible they're simply hikers who took another side trail and were camping at the falls. We're sending people to check on them."

Ed's face registers no emotion whatsoever as he says, "That's good work, Ryan. Good work." More potential witnesses and another crack in Ed's murderous plan. Maybe he's not as good as he thinks he is.

Ryan is about to leave when he stutters in his tracks and turns back. "Say, Ed. What part of the park did you say you were in this morning, anyway?"

Ed is now sitting on his tailgate, slowly undoing the laces of his new hiking shoes. I can see he's scrambling to come up with an answer that Ryan will buy. There's no reason at all for Ryan to be suspicious, and yet, at least to my eyes, Ed reeks of guilt. It's permeating his every pore.

"Closer to home, east of the highway near Fenton-Treeby. Didn't have a lot of time to go very far into the park this morning. Why do you ask?"

"Check out my boots." Ryan is displaying his right standard issue black boot, tilting it from side to side. "I picked up some caked mud from the bogs on my perimeter search at the crime scene. It has the same reddish, grey color that I saw on your boots this morning when I was rolling out the trash."

Ed raises his eyes to find Ryan's. "Ryan, that reddish mud is found all through the park. You know that."

"Yeah, I know, Ed. I was just wondering if it was something we could use as a clue here. I mean, the shooter must have taken the shot from somewhere deep in the woods off the side of the trail. There are creeks and bogs everywhere in there. Thought maybe it could be some additional circumstantial evidence we could nail the bastard with, if we ever catch him ... or her." Ryan has obviously just realized that nut-job snipers come in both flavors, and, although exceedingly rare, the perp could be female.

Ed stands, both of his work shoes now on, looks at Ryan and gives him a fatherly smile. "That's a good line of thinking, Ryan." He reaches down and wipes his index finger along the edge of Ryan's boot, picking up a scoop of mud as if it were peanut butter from a jar. He holds the finger in front of Ryan's face and says, "But, really, you can find this stuff all over the park. It's not something that would tie anyone to the crime scene."

Ryan nods his head unconvincingly, and I can tell he isn't entirely in agreement. Ryan was born in Wawa and has spent his entire life here, other than his three years of police training. Although he doesn't hunt, he's an avid hiker and woodsman. He knows the terrain of Lake Superior Park as well, or better, than Ed. In fact, I wonder if he didn't already know about that connecting trail that Phil is checking out.

Ed abruptly changes the subject and says, "Listen, Ryan. This case is obviously too close to home for me, so I'm signing out full command to you to assist the homicide team as best you can."

"You got it, boss. Are you heading back to the office?"

"No, I'm going straight home. I've got a brutal headache, and I still have to contact Sarah to deliver the terrible news."

Ryan is staring at the ground, kicking a pebble with his muddy boots. "Right. Man. I still can't believe it. Your brother. It's crazy. This is the kind of stuff you read in mystery novels and see in movies. Not the kind of thing that happens in our neck of the woods."

"Appreciate the condolences, Ryan. You're a good friend."

"Well, if you need me, I'll be here. Call you if anything comes up."

Ryan gets back on his ATV. Before gunning it, he turns back to Ed and yells, "We'll get the bastard, Ed."

He then pulls away, wheels spinning, and disappears down the Towab Trail.

Ed gets into his truck and, in contrast to both Ryan and Matt, creeps out of the parking lot ever so slowly, puttering down Frater Road towards the highway, like he's out for a Sunday stroll. It seems that Ed is in no hurry to get anywhere. And why would he be? He has to tell Winona that he has killed his own brother. And he must call Sarah. I can't imagine a more difficult and painful phone call. All the while thinking through over and over again everything he's done. Has he completely covered his tracks? Is there something else at the crime scene he missed? Or, in the woods?

Sarah! Normally, after someone passes, people recite some version of, "Well, he or she is dead. It's a terrible thing, but they're gone. It's the next of kin still alive that are going to suffer." Poor Sarah. So unexpected. She'll never know what hit her. With our daughter, June, past her first year, we were trying for a second child. It took five years of IVF to bring June into this world, and these days we were completely focused on making baby number two. It's possible even now that she's pregnant. A consolation prize for losing her husband? The child I will never meet. Most dead people will never get the chance to ponder this kind of stuff after they're dead. Is this a gift where I get a last chance to see and think through all the good things in my life? Or is this a version of hell where I get to ruminate over everything that has been taken from me?

There is no music playing this time as Ed drives, only tensioned silence. When we arrive at the intersection for the TransCanada Highway, the two officers from this morning are still there, manning the blockade. But there are also several other vehicles present. In particular, a small hatchback from CTV News is parked to the side with a man setting up a camera on a tripod. When he sees the truck approach, he swings the camera excitedly in our direction. My brother is going to be on the evening news. The dedicated cop doing his duty to uncover a grisly murder.

What will the news say when they realize the victim is his own brother?

And what will the headline eventually read when they find out who the killer is?

Chapter 12

4:00 PM

I suddenly find myself floating behind Ryan's ATV, following him as he speeds along the Towab Trail. I'm reminded of the Speeder chase scene in the third Star Wars movie, slaloming around gigantic trees, weaving in and out. Except, it seems, I can travel straight through the trees and everything else with no ill effect, a fringe benefit of being some kind of ghost. This scene in the movie always made me smile from ear to ear. Not so today. I'm once again being brought back to ground zero, where I died. Haven't I seen it enough already? Seriously, is it truly necessary for whatever puppet master running this show to rub my nose in it repeatedly? I take a deep breath, and think, *There must be a good reason. I just have to allow the flow.*

I can see the yellow tape around the trees up ahead, along with the three members of the homicide team, each of them doing a specific task. Everything looks as it did when we left a half hour earlier, except they've got my body in a black bag now – a body bag. At least I won't have to look at my dead self again. There's still a lake of blood marking the former location. I would have expected it to be absorbed into the earth by now. But I remember the trail is very dry and the ground is packed solid from a thousand tread marks over the course of the summer. My blood markings will likely remain until the next rain dilutes and erases them. Ground zero: where my old journey ended and this new one began.

Ryan parks his ATV next to the other one and is standing with a hand on the seat, staring at something far down the trail. My awareness is pulled in that direction and from my levitating vantage point, I see two hikers heading this way. Ryan walks quickly towards them, dodging around the yellow tape. The other investigators haven't noticed the new people yet. For reasons known only to the mystical powers directing this show, I remain at a distance.

Perhaps information I'm not ready to process?

Ryan speaks to them at length, pointing at first to the crime scene and then in various directions in the woods. I can see them clearly, but I can only hear a muddled conversation. The hikers, at first, are clearly shocked. The woman – fit, medium height, mid-twenties, pretty, carrying a light day pack – places a hand on her chest. Her eyes are wide, like a startled doe, as if she's not sure she can believe what she's hearing. The man – also very fit, tall, dark complexion, good looking, carrying a fanny pack – has raised eyebrows hanging like little tents over squinted eyes. He's trying to see past Ryan to get a better view of the crime scene.

His hand keeps reaching into his jacket, like he's trying to find his phone to snap a picture.

There's a lot of nodding and head shaking going on until, ultimately, Ryan escorts them around the crime scene. The members of the forensics team look up at them briefly, nodding hellos like they're at the office, and then return to their work. The eyes of the hikers are glued to the body bag and the red pool of blood, with their heads rotating steadily to keep their gazes directed at the action until they reach the trail on the other side. Ryan seems to be thanking them. He gives them each a business card, the same card he gave Matt in the parking lot. I sense they've told him something important.

Chapter 13

4:00 PM

Like a paraffin candle in a strong breeze, my spectral heart melts away. I'm now looking at Sarah pushing June in a baby carriage along a Bellevue Park path in Sault Ste. Marie – The Soo. I suspect they're heading for the kiddy swings. Sarah is humming obliviously to herself, an old favorite Elton John tune called *Tiny Dancer*. Her voice is much better than she thinks it is, and I'm loving every note. June starts giggling uncontrollably as the swings come into view. It's easily her favorite activity at the park.

It seems like ages since I last saw them but, really, it was just this morning. I think the problem is that I know it will be ages, or maybe even eternity, before I see them again.

Will I ever see them again?

I remember kissing a deep-sleepy Sarah on the cheek before leaving at sunrise this morning. June was snuggled in between us after a difficult night of teething, and I didn't dare disturb her. Already, the memories seem faded … and fading. I guess the dead don't need memories.

Sarah's unwashed brown hair is tied back tightly. She's gone Covid natural, and there's a faint touch of grey showing. I think it makes her look even sexier than her usual blond, but she doesn't believe me. She looks tired. June's new teeth are taking their toll on us … on her.

And I realize, *Christ! Everything going forward is just her and only her.*

My mum is still living in England and, being in her mid-eighties, too old to be of much help. Sarah's parents moved to Toronto to be closer to Sarah's divorced younger sister, who, unfortunately, has a child with severe autism. That just leaves Jenna, her older sister, who still lives here in The Soo. She's also a pharmacist at our hospital and completely reliable. Jenna has always been there for us, and I can only pray she'll be there for Sarah and June now.

Look at me, *praying*. Not something I've done since my church going years in grade school, a time when we attended Catholic mass weekly. Being almost dead does that to a person, I guess. Makes you pray for something … anything.

With school back in session, there are only a few other kids and their relatives spread out sparsely around the park. I'm suddenly reminded of the dire predictions and forecasts of the public health experts. While June may have been one of the first babies to be infected with Covid-19 last December when Omicron was catching fire, the trend has been no less than exponential, as kids returning to school in full force with no protection other than vaccines and hand hygiene have exchanged the virus to such an extent that entire classrooms and schools have already been shut down. The trickle down effects have been even worse as the children bring the virus home and pass it on to their parents, who pass it on to their relatives and work colleagues, who pass it on to ….

Even worse is the early upswing in RSV and influenza A cases being seen. Hypothesized to be either: 1. A secondary and unexpected consequence of isolating ourselves over the past three years and under stimulation of our immune systems, or 2. A secondary and unexpected effect of the Covid virus itself. Experts continue to debate endlessly with no definitive answers forthcoming. Much as we all want answers now, the reality is that science is slow and methodical work, and, as my friend Hitchhiker once told me, by the time we get the answers to most of these kinds of questions, we will likely have moved on to some other world catastrophe.

Sarah pushes the baby carriage up to the kiddy swings, the kind where you can slip the legs in with a "seat belt" to keep everything safe. Before she gets there, she stops prematurely, eliciting a protest cry from June. Sarah is looking towards the big kid swings and focused on one particularly large "kid." She then redirects the baby carriage and yells, "Rebecca?"

Rebecca is arcing big time. Some twenty or more feet off the ground at either end of the swing pendulum. Her gaze is directed towards outer space. Eventually she hears Sarah calling and looks in her direction. A big smile spreads across her face when she spots the baby carriage. She is June's biggest fan. The only baby in our little, spread-out tribe.

Her swing gently returns to earth, and she quickly climbs off and runs to Sarah and June.

"Juuuuuuune! Baby Juuuune!"

Rebecca is giddy with joy and has June unbuckled and lifted high in the air before Sarah can get a word out. With their googly eyes locked in sync, Rebecca is dancing in circles, centrifuging June as if she's on a playground spinner. Pure joy.

They finally come to a stop and, with a dizzy, vibrating June in her arms, Rebecca steps over to hug Sarah. There's a weird Covid hesitation, since they live in different cities, but ultimately the trio embrace. It's been many months since they've seen each other.

"What in the world are you doing here, Rebecca? I thought you were still at Stanford?" Sarah asks with one hand still on Rebecca's shoulder and one hand on June's.

"I am," Rebecca responds. "But with a semester left in my PhD, it's all computer work at this point. And with all the Covid stuff going on, it's just easier to work from home."

"You're back home, living with your parents?"

"Nope. Not this time. I really needed to focus, so I rented an apartment all to myself until December."

"After that?" Sarah asks.

"That will depend on how my thesis goes."

"And how is it going?"

"Really good, actually. In fact, my supervisor called this morning after going over a first draft. He said I may be on track to win a Nobel prize!"

"Seriously? A Nobel prize? No one wins one of those out of Grad school. That's amazing."

"Small glitch, though. One of my key formulas has an error in it."

"Uh-oh. Fatal?"

"That's what I'm trying to figure out. I drove from Wawa trying to get inspired. Driving helps me think."

"Apparently, swinging helps you think, also." Sarah says, eyeing the "big kid" swing set.

"It has in the past but not this time. I can't seem to get it. It's like the answer is right there for me to grab, and I just can't latch on. Even the follow-up email from my supervisor didn't help."

"Wait. Is this the same thesis that has to do with the −?"

"Shhh." Rebecca puts an index to her smiling lips, whereupon June mimics her and giggles. "My supervisor told me to keep it under wraps. I'm not supposed to talk about it with anyone anymore. He said big pharma would be all over this if they found out."

"Wow. That's very exciting. Swear, I won't tell a soul."

"Where's your hubby these days?" Rebecca asks. "Off on another crazy adventure?"

"Just the garden variety Wawa style. He drove up this morning to do a shift in the ER at Lady Dunn Hospital."

"Kayaking as well?" Rebecca asks.

"Hiking, I believe. He left at sunrise and was planning a stop at the Agawa pictographs before work."

"Is he staying overnight?"

"Yes, I think he's staying with your parents and doing one more shift tomorrow before coming home."

"Perfect. My parents invited me for dinner tonight. I can see my uncle as well. It's been a while."

"Maybe he can help jog your mind to figure out your formula. He's very good that way.

"Hopefully, you're right."

The whole scene reminds me of the "Ghost of Christmas Present" scene in the Dickens classic *A Christmas Carol*. I'm beyond ecstatic at seeing my wife and child, as well as seeing Rebecca again, but I hate the significance of that story. Is there a lesson I need to learn here? If there is, to what point? I'm dead ... aren't I?

Rebecca finally says goodbye to Sarah and June. She gets back into her SUV and heads home to Wawa. If she's anxious to talk to me at dinner about her thesis, she will be greatly disappointed.

Chapter 14

5:30 PM

Ed is sitting slouched on the edge of his living room couch with his elbows propped on his knees and his hands supporting his jaw. He's staring at his phone parked on the coffee table directly in front of him. Next to his phone is the bottle of bourbon. There is no glass. He looks beyond miserable. The TV mounted on the far wall is showing the news, but the volume is off.

"I can't do it," he says.

"*You* are the staff sergeant. It's your duty. She has to know." Winona says, forcefully.

"Dammit, Win, she's my brother's wife. A man should never have to call his brother's wife to tell her about her husband's death."

No doubt Winona and I are thinking the same thing, *especially when you are the one who killed him.*

It appears I've arrived a little late to this party. Ed has obviously already told Winona that I was the

73

victim, and the news has had a profound effect on her. There is a quiver in her chin that I've never seen before and, while she's trying to be supportive of her husband, her voice is flat and lacks its usual color. She's sitting on a chair across from Ed, nursing, what appears to be, a cup of tea with a trembling hand. Winona has never touched alcohol. She reaches across for the bottle.

"This isn't making it any easier for you."

Before she can pull it off the coffee table, Ed grabs it.

"I need it. Right now, I really need it."

"There's a lot at stake, Ed. You need to have a clear mind."

"I pulled myself off the case. No one will fault me for getting a little drunk under the circumstances."

"I'm not sure that was the right thing to do. Ryan's not as dumb as you think he is."

"He'll never be staff sergeant. He doesn't have what it takes." Ed's tongue is thickening as the bourbon bottle steadily empties.

"Don't be so sure."

There's a long moment of empty silence before Ed picks up his phone.

I'm dreading this call, probably more than my brother is.

He hesitates for a few seconds, trying to focus on the screen, and then taps Sarah's phone number. She picks up after the second ring.

"Hey, Ed," she answers, "how are you? Is my silly, vagabonding husband there yet? I assume he's staying over?"

Ed has his phone in both hands and is pushing it into his forehead as he rocks forwards and backwards on the edge of the couch. Finally, he blurts out in one breath, "Sarah … I have something horrible to tell you. Mark was found dead this morning on the Towab Trail. He was shot. We don't know by who or for what reason but … he's dead. My brother, your husband, is dead."

Something seems to give inside Ed's mind as he makes this last statement. The rocking resumes.

"Fuck off, Ed. Did Mark put you up to this? He's such an asshole sometimes. You guys are both into the sauce, aren't you? And I thought you were on the wagon. Put him on the damn phone, so I can chew him out properly."

Ed suddenly stands up and is staring at the TV. He can read the subtitled headlines: Breaking news – *Local doctor found shot to death on hiking trail in Lake Superior Park.*

"Sarah, I'm so, so sorry. It's all true. Turn on the CTV News. Mark's not here. He's not coming back …"

"What?"

I can hear the emotion building in Sarah's voice.

"This isn't funny anymore, Ed. Put Mark on, *now*."

Ed's face is changing. It looks crooked somehow, like he's unraveling. He's swaying a little. The booze is smothering him.

There's a pause on the phone. Presumably, Sarah is turning on the news. She comes back online, "Ed, what the fuck's going on? Who's the doctor that was killed?"

"Sarah … I'm trying to tell you. This isn't a joke. It was Mark."

This is where I die, again. When Sarah realizes that I'm really dead. I can't feel pain and yet I do. Every ghostly atom of whatever it is I am is crying out in torment. My poor Sarah …

"It's impossible, Ed. There's no way Mark's dead. He was just on his way to work going for a healthy hike. Who would want to kill him … no one would want to kill him … would they? It's impossible …?"

"It's all true," is all Ed can say.

There's a high pitched wail of anguish coming from Ed's phone that's too much for him to bear. He drops it on the floor and then falls to his knees with his head buried in his hands. "What have I done!" he wails uncontrollably.

A heel comes down hard on the phone: Winona's heel. She pulverizes Ed's phone into silence.

"Hopefully, she didn't hear that," Winona says calmly, more in control. She places a hand on his back and rubs it in a circular motion, as one would do for a colicky baby. "You need to pull it together, husband. Rebecca will be here any moment. I'll call Sarah back on my phone to console her. I'll tell her you're too broken up to talk to her anymore."

Winona is a strong woman, who'd faced abusive and life threatening adversity repeatedly prior to meeting my brother. She has the willpower and courage to push through anything. Now, though, she's walking a very thin tightrope requiring more balance and finesse than sheer determination and willpower. Ed has done something that she can't condone, something that violates every direction of her moral compass, yet she won't abandon him. She will do whatever it takes to keep him safe. To protect their love. Even if it means diving into his world to bring him back.

She crouches down to be at Ed's level, squeezes his face with a hand on either side, and then tilts his head up to make eye contact. I can see Ed's eyes, but I'm not sure anyone's home.

"I don't agree with what you did. But remember why you did it: to save Rebecca's life."

This sparks Ed back to life, and his bleary eyes open scarily wide, like he's had an epiphany. He stands. "Did I? Did I really save her life?"

"Of course, you did. As you said, she probably would have died in that car accident."

"According to some crazy vision I had. Even so. Even if the vision were true, what makes her life more valuable than Mark's?"

This is the million dollar question. After hearing Sarah's voice on the phone, I'm wondering the same thing.

Why is Rebecca's life more valuable than mine?

"She's our daughter," Winona responds.

Sarah, June, my mum, my patients ... I don't think being his daughter is enough anymore.

There's a knock and then the door to the side of the house slowly opens.

Chapter 15

6:20 PM

"Mother? Father?" Rebecca yells, standing just inside the threshold.

"Ed," Winona whispers, "go to the bathroom and fix yourself up. We have to tell Rebecca about Mark ... but nothing more. Okay? Not yet."

Ed has that dulled, closed look on his face once again, like there's too much going on in his outside world to allow him to process what's going on in his inside world.

"Ed?" Winona shakes his shoulder.

His eyes stir a little. "Right. Yeah. Okay, I'll get cleaned up."

"Good. I'll try and get some dinner ready."

Winona is turning to enter the kitchen, and Ed has one foot going upstairs, when Rebecca materializes in front of them. It couldn't be more awkward timing. She's carrying her backpack on one shoulder with a bottle in a brown liquor bag tucked under her armpit. She's vibrating with excitement.

"Hey, Mom and Dad. Have you been following the news? Dad, you must know something about the doctor shot and killed on the Towab Trail. It's crazy. There's even a photo going viral on social media showing the body. It's like something from one of my murder mystery podcasts."

Rebecca pauses to take a long breath and, for the first time, seems to be noticing her parents aren't quite right.

"Shit. Dad, you look horrible. And you reek of booze. What the hell? Shouldn't you be involved in the case? It's part of your jurisdiction, isn't it?

If it was possible for Ed's shoulders to slump any closer to the floor, they did. He removes his one foot from the stair and plants both feet on the floor. He looks at Winona, who then says, "Rebecca, come into the kitchen. We have something horrible to tell you."

"What? What's going on? Is it somebody I know?"

"Just sit down and we'll talk."

The table is set for dinner with placemats and cutlery. All done before Ed dropped the second bomb on her, the one about my being the victim. I'm sure the last thing on Winona's weary mind is dinner. They each pull out their respective, usual chairs and sit. Well, Rebecca isn't exactly sitting. One leg is folded under her buttocks, and she's bouncing nervously in place. Ed pushes the placemat and cutlery away to make room for his hands which are fidgeting with each other. He tries to speak but comes up short every time. He looks to Winona once again for support.

"Well …? Tell me," Sarah pleads.

"Honey," Winona begins, "the doctor that died this morning was your Uncle Mark."

The bouncing stops abruptly. "Uncle Mark? Noooooooo. It can't be. Rebecca has both hands covering her mouth now. "How … Why?"

"Just as the news is reporting, he was shot and killed. No one knows why at this point."

Pretty sure we know why. It was to save you, Rebecca.

"But … you must know something."

"He was doing one of his typical morning-before-work hikes on the Towab Trail, and then …"

"Damn." Rebecca is shaking her head from side to side. "I was just with Sarah and June a few hours ago. Does she know?"

"Your father spoke to her before you walked through the door. That's why he's … struggling right now."

Winona, who's sitting next to Ed, puts a comforting hand on his neck. Rebecca reaches across the table to place her hands over her father's. "Dad, I'm so sorry. This is so incredibly wrong. I mean, Uncle Mark was the best guy ever."

"Ed," Winona says gently, almost whispering, "why don't you go upstairs to the bathroom and take a moment. Get cleaned up for … for dinner."

As if dinner means anything now.

Ed doesn't utter a word. He just nods his head, gets up from the table, and leaves. He stumbles up the stairs to the bathroom. I'm following him and can hear Winona offering Rebecca something to drink and Rebecca saying she brought a sparkly to celebrate her almost finished thesis, but she doesn't want it now. There's the sound of sobbing as the reality cuts hard into Rebecca.

When Ed reaches the top of the stairs, he pauses to catch his breath and then goes straight to the bathroom. He flicks the light on and closes the door. He stares at himself in the mirror and at first seems startled by his appearance. He squeezes his eyes closed; his hands are braced on either side of the sink cabinet. One hand then reaches down to his pistol, and he rubs his hand over the cold metal. He forgot to leave his pistol hanging at the entrance.

Or did he?

He releases the safety snap on his holster. A long moment passes, and then he sits down on the toilet lid. He stares at the wall for a few moments and then slowly draws the pistol from his holster, unclicks the safety, and places the tip of the barrel under his chin.

I'm freaking out. I'm not a big believer in a life for a life. It shatters my heart to think that my entire family is about to be destroyed, and there's nothing I can do to stop it.

A voice cries out from downstairs, "Dad? Dad, are you okay up there? Come down for dinner."

Ed's hands begin to tremble, and the gun barrel oscillates in a circular motion. He opens his eyes and lifts the gun barrel to eye level, looking straight into it, straight down the barrel. He releases a heavy sigh and mumbles, "I have to tell her. Why I did it ... to save her."

He stands and holsters his weapon. He takes a towel and wipes the sheen of sweat off his forehead and then cups his hands under the tap, taking a sip before splashing water over his face.

He looks into the mirror. "Time to sober up."

Another deep breath, and then he opens the door and descends the stairs. His steps have a little bounce in them and look more purposeful. The guilt is eating him alive, and I can tell he's decided to tell Rebecca the truth.

Ed enters the kitchen, and Rebecca immediately wraps him in a big, comforting hug. He smiles for a moment but then pushes her away to arm's distance and keeps her there.

"Rebecca, there's something more I have to tell you."

Winona is moving dishes around at the sink, almost randomly, trying to occupy herself, but stops midmotion when she hears this. She tries to catch Ed's eye. He's avoiding her gaze.

He clears his throat and begins, "The night before last, I started having these weird dreams. I tossed and turned all night, waking up over and over. You know me. I'm usually a deep sleeper, and I never have dreams. At least, dreams that I can remem –"

"– Ed," Winona pleads, "Rebecca doesn't need to know this."

Ed suddenly sends a wild, determined look in Winona's direction and yells, "Hell, yes, she does!"

His hand is resting on his pistol holster, and Rebecca takes a step back. There's a determined, fierce, carnal look on his face.

Winona raises both her hands in supplication and cries, "It's not just *your* life. It's our life. All of ours."

Ed shakes his head and yells. "It's too late, way too late."

Rebecca squints and whispers, "What the hell are you two going on about?"

Ed looks to his daughter once more and continues, "When I got out of bed yesterday morning to go to work, I was tired as hell. I could barely keep my eyes open. But every time I closed them, the same dream would start up again. And then it started happening even when my eyes were open, and I was awake, my mind swimming with weird ideas that weren't my own. It was like there was someone else in my head who had dropped a screen over my eyes, showing me a terrible home movie on a loop. It gave me a brutal headache, like the worst migraine you could imagine, and blurred my eyes. I slammed into the wall in our bedroom and damn near fell down the stairs. I had your mother call me in sick. You know me. I haven't missed a day of work in a decade. I went back to bed, and it kept going all day and right into last –"

"Mom," Rebecca interrupts, glaring at her. "Why didn't you take him to the hospital? He may have been having a seizure, or a stroke, or something?"

Winona looks gaunt and defeated, like she's fighting an unwinnable war. She shrugs her shoulders and replies, "I didn't know. He told me he just had a bad headache and needed to take the day off … I didn't know. I gave him some Tylenol and –"

"And then they just … stopped," Ed says. He's staring out the kitchen window now, his eyes flittering here and there, not focused on anything in particular. "Just like that, almost exactly at midnight, twenty-four hours after they started, the visions disappeared, and I

83

was left with this imprint in my head, something the visions told me I had to do."

"Visions?" Rebecca asks, blinking repeatedly.

Winona is shaking her head meekly from side to side. She whispers, "I keep telling you, Ed. Those weren't visions. They were something different ...."

Rebecca nods her head almost imperceptibly. Her arms are crossed in front of her protectively, and there's now a look of frightened bewilderment on her face. Rebecca is familiar with her heritage and with visions. She's had a few herself over the years. "Dad, you're scaring me. What? What were these so called visions? Where is this going?"

Ed takes another deep breath. He's getting to the difficult part. "The visions told me that you would die in a car accident."

"What? How? Where?"

"The intersection, Mission Road and Winston."

"The one under construction? With the temporary signal lights?"

"Yes. That one. This morning at 10:18 AM."

Rebecca thinks for a moment and then says, "I was around that area this morning."

"You were exactly at that intersection this morning at 10:18 AM."

"But ... nothing happened."

"That's right, nothing happened," Ed confirms.

"What was supposed to happen? According to your visions?"

"A man, on his way to work, would have seen a malfunctioning green light and accidentally rammed your truck, killing you."

"What? That's crazy!"

"It's what the visions showed me over and over again."

"Wait. What does this have to do with Uncle Mark?"

"He would have been the driver."

"So … what? It never happened because some psycho shot and killed Uncle Mark. Why would someone …?"

Rebecca, my super intelligent niece, instantly connects all the dots. She backs all the way into the kitchen wall.

"YOU? You shot Uncle Mark? YOU killed him?"

Ed looks like *he's* been shot, hearing her daughter say it out loud. The pure and deadly truth of it. He staggers and his body sags as if his blood has leaked out. All he can say is, "I did it to save your life."

"You killed your own brother, my only uncle, based on a … on a cockamamie dream vision."

Rebecca looks to her mother again. "Mom? You know about this?"

Winona once again nods her head meekly. "He told me this morning before he left the house. I thought he was going in early to work. I never thought he'd …"

A suffocating silence descends over their little kitchen.

"Have both of you completely lost your minds?"

Rebecca's pointing her finger at Ed now. "You're the staff sergeant for God's sake. And you killed your own brother?"

Winona looks confused. Unsure what to say. She believes in her husband, and she believes in visions, but she would never stake someone's life on it. And she's quite sure what happened to Ed was not a vision. Still, she defends him. "Rebecca, honey, you know visions can be powerful and real."

"Oh, Dad's visions were real all right. Real nutso. Geezus, why did you even tell me this? They weren't even visions they were … something else. Hallucinations? Delusions? A psychotic break, maybe?"

She has both hands now clasped over her temples. "How is this supposed to make me feel? I loved Uncle Mark, he was awesome. He was always there when I needed him. Fuuuck! This is first degree murder!!"

Rebecca moves her hands over her ears, like she's trying to unhear everything her dad has told her.

"Look, I can't take any more of this … whatever this is. I mean, what am I supposed to do? Turn you in? Look the other way, and pretend I never heard any of it? Commit you to a mental ward?"

There's another miserable silence broken only by the sound of water boiling on the stove. Winona has turned her back, ostensibly dealing with the dinner. Ed is standing repentant with his palms out, like a guilty man waiting for judgement.

Rebecca's voice is scarily calm. "I love you both, but I need some space to process this and decide what I'm going to do next. Don't worry. I'm not going to turn you in. At least not until I've thought it through. I mean, I get that you were trying to save my life, but this is all so … insane."

Rebecca turns, grabs her backpack off a chair, and then marches out the side door, never looking back.

I hear her SUV fire up and squeal out of the driveway. I don't know for sure where she's going, but I can guess.

Ed collapses to the floor once again with his head in his hands, sobbing.

What did he think was going to happen? That Rebecca would completely understand and say, "Thanks, Dad. You're awesome for saving my life."

Winona doesn't know what to do with herself. She's still taking care of a dinner that no one will eat. She looks at Ed intermittently but makes no attempt to console him. She has her own inner struggles to deal with. Her love for her husband, her soulmate, has always been a core aspect of her being, but can she really live with what he's done?

Winona's cell phone rings, and she reflexively picks it up.

"Winona? It's Ryan. Is Ed there? He's not answering his cell, and I need to talk to him right away. I'm next door. I'm coming over."

Chapter 16

6:40 PM

The kitchen side door opens after a brief knock. A voice yells, "Ed? Winona? It's Ryan."

Ryan enters and glances at the vacant brass hook next to the door, the one where Ed's firearm is normally kept. He purses his lips and yells again, "Hello?"

"In the living room, Ryan," Winona yells back.

Ryan looks twitchy. His hand is resting on his firearm. He knows something, and he's not happy he knows it.

He walks up the stairs and into the kitchen. He sees through the door into the living room, where Ed is now sitting in a recliner chair staring at the floor, and Winona is standing behind him, massaging his shoulders.

"You weren't answering your phone."

Ed tilts his head to the floor where the remnants of his phone still lay in tatters.

Ryan steps to the threshold of the living room and looks to the floor. "Oh. That explains it."

He doesn't ask why Ed's phone is lying in pieces on the floor.

"Was that Rebecca I saw speeding away?"

"We told her about Mark," Winona says. She doesn't mention the part about Ed killing me. "She was very upset and had to sort herself out."

"Right. Poor kid …"

"What's up, Ryan? News about the investigation?" asks Winona.

Ryan is standing in the doorway with one foot in the kitchen and one foot in the living room, shifting his weight uncomfortably from one to the other. He looks like he'd rather be anywhere but here.

"Sort of." He takes a deep breath and says, "Ed, I have three questions I have to ask you."

Ed looks up for the first time. His eyes are bloodshot and drawn. Tears are tracking from each corner down his cheeks. He looks like he's aged a dozen years since he killed me this morning. He doesn't say anything.

Ryan pushes on. "Ed, did you take the patrol boat out this morning? Buck, from the marina, called me. He'd heard about the murder and, seeing the patrol boat go out around lunchtime – after the murder, was wondering if there was a connection. If maybe another body was found or something? His imagination was running pretty wild. I checked the logbook on the boat but there's nothing. Was that you?"

Ed leans back in the recliner and says, "It was me. I didn't have any luck hunting this morning, so I thought I'd get an hour of fishing in before heading to work."

I'm impressed. Ed seems to have pulled himself together, again. *He's like the Jekyll and Hyde of guilt and innocence.*

"I must have forgotten to fill out the logbook."

"That's not like you, Ed. You're a by the books kind of guy. Always have been."

This is completely true and one of the reasons that my brother has done so well with his career in the police force.

"I forgot. What can I say. Guess I've had some stuff on my mind."

An understatement.

"Okay. Next question: Where did you say you were hunting this morning?"

"We've already had this discussion, Ryan." There's a note of irritation in Ed's voice now.

"Humor me, Ed"

"Fenton-Treeby, like I told you earlier. Is this about the mud on my boots again?"

Ryan now steps completely into the living room. "When I went back to the crime scene, after I left you in the parking lot, two hikers showed up. They had parked further up Frater Road and hiked the loop to Burnt Rock Pool via an accessory trail, returning on the Towab Trail."

"Did they hear or see something?" Ed asks.

"Nothing around the crime scene, but they did see a large black police pickup exiting Frater Road going north when they arrived from The Soo around

9:15 AM. They were surprised the police were making rounds so early, particularly when it's usually Conservation Officers that do that kind of thing. Their description matches your pickup completely."

Ed is averting eye contact now, and Winona has stopped massaging his shoulders and is simply standing there, helplessly watching everything unfold.

"Mine is not the only pickup cruiser on the road, Ryan. Could have been someone else. Even someone from The Soo."

"Except that it rained yesterday, and we lifted a set of tire tracks from the Sewage Lagoon parking area. So, we know the tracks are fresh and from today. They belong to a set of off-road Pirelli Scorpions, like the ones on your truck. Not very common."

Ed's eyes are darting around until he finally looks up and to the left. He's trying to access the creative part of his brain but coming up empty. He gives Ryan a crooked smile and supinates both hands into a supplicating gesture.

"Alright, Ryan. You got me. I was hunting in that area this morning. As we both know, it's illegal to hunt in the park. Once I heard about the murder, I knew there would be questions and word would get out. I didn't think it would look good for the department. We all hunt in the park. It's an understood perk of the job, plus it allows us to keep an eye for poachers, helping out our CO colleagues."

There's a pause and then Ryan asks, "And you never heard a shot? I mean, based on the hiker's report, you were there around the time of your brother's murder. You must have heard something?"

Ed is shifting very uncomfortably in his chair. "Look, I may have heard … something." For the first time, Ed's not lying. Of course, he heard something. The rifle was inches away from his ears when he shot me.

"But I was in my truck and had the music on. I couldn't be sure. Again, I didn't want people to know I was there. For the good of the department."

Ryan's eyes widen, and his hands fly into the air. "For Pete's sake, Ed, your brother was shot and killed, and you're worried about violating some hunting laws?"

Ryan is visibly upset now and takes another step closer. Winona tries to place her hands back on Ed's shoulders, but he waves her off. He's Mr. Hyde again, and he's got that deranged look, like Jack Nicholson in The Shining.

"What's your thiiiird question, Ryaaan!" He spits out venomously.

Ryan takes a half step backwards. He looks scared. "Sarah called me about an hour ago. She wanted to confirm what you'd told her. She still couldn't believe it. She was still hoping desperately that you and Mark might have been pranking her. She was hard to understand through all the tears, but she was very clear on this. She wanted to know what you meant by, 'What have I done?'"

Winona, upon hearing this, immediately retreats to the wall, behind and to the side of the recliner chair. Ironically, she's standing next to a large photo of Ed and I, taken about twenty years ago. We're both dressed in fishing gear, and he has a big arm over my shoulder. We're both radiating toothy smiles as we hold up a huge catch of salmon. And just under this photo, resting on a small end table, is a hardcover children's book called *The Adventures of Geekboy* I'd written and published years earlier when Rebecca was barely in grade school. I remembered Ed being so proud of his brilliant and precocious little Rebecca reading aloud a book written by his little brother, the budding author.

Bright lights suddenly illuminate the living room through the windows facing the driveway. There's a flash of blue and red and the squeal of brakes.

The tension in the air is so thick it's hard even for me to breathe – and I have no lungs. Ed abruptly rocks forward from the recliner and stands. In one smooth motion, he draws his pistol. At exactly the same moment, Ryan does the same. It's like watching an old west gunslinger quick draw.

They are standing less than eight feet apart both aiming their pistols at each other. Ryan is rock solid with both feet planted like hundred-year-old elms. Ed is swaying, as if he's standing on the Titanic. Ed breaks eye contact to look at Winona. Ryan could take him down easily at this point, but he doesn't. Ed has been Ryan's colleague, close friend, and mentor for more than a decade.

Ed looks confused, angry, pleading, all at the same time. And then he smiles.

He turns to look at Ryan apologetically, like he's failed him, and closes his eyes. He then slowly puts the barrel of his pistol against his temple.

Winona cries out something unintelligible as she grabs her face with both hands and turns her head into the wall.

Ryan yells, "This isn't the way, Ed. Just tell me, why? Was it to do with your mortgage? Paying back the money you owed Mark? Why else would you do such a thing?"

"You can't understand, Ryan. It had nothing to do with money. I did it to save my daughter."

Just as Ed begins to squeeze the trigger, Ryan shoots. The bullet enters Ed's upper right chest just below his clavicle. It's a brilliant shot aimed directly at Ed's brachial plexus, the nerves that control his arm. It's nonlethal and the blast disrupts the nerve signals running from Ed's brain to his gun hand. His arm slumps paralysed to his side, and the gun drops to the floor. He falls back into the recliner chair and buries his face in his one remaining hand, sobbing uncontrollably as he rocks forwards and backwards. Winona runs to him and holds him tightly.

He whispers through his tears over and over, "I can't tell what's real anymore."

***

The aftermath is chaotic as policemen from the squad cars outside pile in from both the front and the side doors. They are all wearing custom police force issued black face masks that make them look scary as hell. This is offset, however, by the incredulous looks in their eyes. Wawa is a small town where everyone knows everyone, and they've all been here before for social events. Seeing their boss and his wife in such a state affects them deeply. They don't bother handcuffing Ed or Winona. Someone wraps a temporary dressing on Ed's bullet wound. Ryan barks orders and they escort them outside and into one of the squad cars. There's a gathering of neighbors watching on. Within the hour the entire town will know that the head of their local police force was arrested for the murder of his own brother. By tomorrow, it will likely be national news.

I should feel happy and vindicated, relieved that my killer was brought to justice, but I don't. It just hurts, like the same bullet that went through Ed's shoulder found its way into my heart. My brother's life is ruined. Regardless of the outcome, he will never work as a cop again. I have no idea what will happen to Winona, but I'm certain she will stand by him.

I don't understand the vision thing, and I still don't understand why Rebecca's life is worth more than mine. Was Ed's vision real or something concocted in his imagination, a psychotic break? Did something trigger him? No doubt he will get off on an insanity plea. Any decent lawyer will see to that. Was he really insane, though?

I suppose, whether or not the visions were real, no one ever said there wouldn't be consequences. There is still a price to be paid, even if it's sacred magic.

And I've paid the ultimate price.

Chapter 17

7:30 PM

I'm now in the passenger seat of Rebecca's SUV. My head is still spinning from the events at my brother's house. At first, I'm panicking, and if I could hyperventilate, I would. But, again, I have no lungs. In fact, I'm more like the air inside someone's lungs than the actual lungs, an invisible cloud at Rebecca's side. And then a surreal calmness comes over me, the panic fades, and I feel like an objective observer again. An hour has gone by since Rebecca left her parents. She's staring straight ahead, past the horizon into infinity. There are dried tear tracks on her cheeks and a crust on the back of her hands. We pass a sign indicating the turn off for the Agawa Pictographs and Rebecca pulls into the parking lot.

Uncharacteristically, there's not another vehicle in the parking lot. I wonder if this is by divine design. Normally, this lot would be packed with cars, trailers and even buses. Everyone here to experience a stunning sunset on sacred land. And this really is *sacred land.* The Agawa Rockface was believed to be used as a "stone canvas" by the Ojibwe for two thousand years before European traders paddled the waters of Lake Superior exchanging furs. The current pictographs are estimated to be up to four hundred years old and are painted with red ochre on the massive, flat rockface of Agawa Rock, bordering, and even dipping into, the waters of Gitchee Gumee, or Lake Superior as it is more generally known. A pictograph may contain multiple images including animals such as moose or bears, mythical creatures such as the fish-like Aadzokanaa Gilgoonh, or a Myeengun war party with an eagle, crane, and turtle. It may also have multiple meanings, such as a totem symbol tying an Ojibwe child to the natural world.

Rebecca exits her vehicle and takes off at a quick pace, carrying a good-sized notebook in her right hand, a notebook she carries everywhere. There's a sign indicating the main entrance to the path and a distance of four hundred meters to the pictographs. There's also a connecting path to the Coastal Trail that runs for forty kilometers along the rugged coastline of Lake Superior. Rebecca bypasses all of this and proceeds across the parking lot to another entrance, or rather exit. The pictographs are so popular that there are two separate paths that keep busy foot traffic moving steadily in a counterclockwise direction. The only indication that there's a path here is a sign that indicates no dogs allowed; you have to know it's here.

She bounds along the well beaten path, passing the south entrance to the coastal trail, until she arrives at a long set of stone steps that descend into a crevasse with walls a hundred feet high and an arm's width apart. There's a strong scent of aged moss that creeps up portions of the walls. It's getting dark, the high walls shutting out the light, but I know she's taken these steps regularly since she was a child and descends them two and three at a time with the confidence of a mountain goat.

She stops at one point to place her hand on a palm sized, shell-shaped carving into the stone wall. She closes her eyes for a moment and looks up to the dusky sky, like she's asking for permission to be here. She then pulls an offering of tobacco from a leather pouch she keeps in the pocket of her hiking jacket and sprinkles it around the steps. This is deeply embedded in the heritage taught by her mother, and Rebecca does this habitually as an offering to the sacred land for whatever guidance or inspiration she may receive.

She then continues her journey and before long reaches the intersection to the common path leading to the water's edge and the pictographs. She has a sheen on her brow, and she's breathing heavily, however, her steps seem lighter now, like she's shaken off some of the despair of the last few hours.

Long before we see Lake Superior, we hear it. Winds are high and the sound of crashing waves is unmistakable. At several points along the trail, there are signs enlightening hikers to the dangers of the area; the risks of being swept off the rocks to your death. Several tourists have died in this fashion.

As we approach the waterfront, the trees and vegetation give way to large, craggy blocks of stone turned on edge. Except for the path we are following made up of flat stones secured with concrete, it looks like a giant has stepped on a mountain of stone, and we are walking through the crumbled debris.

She works her way along the path until she is standing in front of a man-made steel railing overlooking a narrow path that descends to the shoreline. Where the railing ends, there's a long inclined area of stone that disappears into the waters of Gitchee Gumee. This inclined stone forms a standing area that wraps around the base of the rockface where the pictographs are located at roughly eye level. Steel bolts with rings are secured at regular intervals into the stone with long hemp ropes attached. Something tourists can latch onto if they are swept into the lake by an unexpected wave – if they are dumb enough to chance a glance at the pictographs on a windy day like today with waves beating the rockface, like a Norse god's hammer.

Rebecca stares first at the area of the pictographs and then at the sun that is sitting like an orb just above the horizon, basking the whole shoreline in a weird, orange glow. She then turns away from the water and looks up at another part of the rockface that is behind her. More particularly, she is looking at a large, ragged stone that is perched all alone on a ledge that's about the width of a narrow balcony. Somehow, the stone looks like its glowing, like the sun is transferring a rainbow of celestial energy to it.

I know this stone intimately. It's a favorite place I visit to set my thoughts in order when I'm in this neck of the woods. I was planning to stop by after my hike on the Towab Trail this morning before work.

Work. It appears I'm going to be a little late for my shift.

Permanently late.

It's a steep climb to get to this stone, but there's another safer way behind a group of cedars with roots locked into the rocks. I showed Rebecca this sitting stone when she was twelve and the safer way to get to it. She climbs in a different direction where there are sharp edged stones embedded, easy to get a foothold. She then works her way along the "path" behind the cedars until she gets to an angled, thick stone wall that acts like a natural wall to the "balcony." When there's even a light drizzle this can be very dangerous, but we've had blue skies all day and, with the heavy winds, everything is bone-dry. She three-points her way over the wall and is standing on the ledge for a moment, taking in the spectacular view of Lake Superior and the setting sun, before she takes a seat on the stone.

There is nothing about this rugged stone that looks in any way inviting. It appears to have sharp, undulating edges in all directions and yet, when you sit on it, somehow the sharpness folds away and it takes you in, like it's tailored to fit.

Rebecca appears out of sorts at first, and it takes a few minutes for her breathing to settle and her shoulders to relax. She pulls the notebook from the small of her back, where it was tucked in by the belt of her jeans for the climb. She places it in her lap and then closes her eyes. She's meditating, trying to find her way through the tangled neurons of her mind created by her father's actions.

She has a blank look on her face, and her dark skin appears bronzed in the glow of the dying sun. I'm standing at her side, wondering if that was the same blank look I would get on my face when I was meditating. There's absolutely no movement anywhere in her body; it's as if she's paralysed.

Within the blink of an eye, as if the puppet master has released all the strings, she collapses and begins to fall forward off the stone and over the edge. I reflexively reach out, but my hand passes right through her. Before she topples off the rockface, her eyes spring wide open. She's in motion, staring straight into the drop before her. Somehow, I can see her face. I'm beside her, in front of her. I'm everywhere and nowhere all at the same time. As she falls, she reaches back with one hand and grabs one of the edges on the stone. It has the shape of a handle, like it was made for exactly this purpose, to save yourself from tumbling to your death.

Her legs have slid out and are hanging over the edge. Her one arm is holding all of her bodyweight. Fortunately, she's very slim and athletic and is able to pull herself back onto the ledge. She immediately sits herself back down on the stone, like all of the acrobatics never happened. Her eyes are still wide open, and she's trembling, but I don't think it's from her near fall, it's something else.

Her hands are moving frantically in all directions, searching. She's looking for …

Her notebook?

She finds it laying at the base of the stone she's sitting on. Another few inches and it would have gone over the edge. She picks it up and wipes a few colorful fall leaves off it. She takes the pen out of a slot on the inside cover and then quickly turns to a blank page. As she flips through, I can see page after page of formulae and genetic sequencing. On the last page, one particular string of genetic coding, part of a larger coding structure, is circled in red with a large question mark next to it. This must be the problem area that she's been working on. She quickly writes down a series of genetic codes, a mixture of the four nitrogenous bases: Adenine, Guanine, Cytosine and Thymine. She writes and writes, flipping page after page, until she stops, and her pen is hovering an inch or so above the page. She takes a deep breath, finishes with a double exclamation mark and then let's out a loud "Whoop" that's immediately swallowed up by the sounds of the waves.

"I've got it. I've freaking got it."

What! What does she have? What could be so important that my life has been sacrificed for this moment?

I look at the sun that has crested the watery horizon and feel like I'm running out of time.

She closes her notebook and lays it on the ground. She stands slowly to take in the view, and it looks like the weight of the world has been lifted from her shoulders.

I'm drawn to her notebook. I need to know what I died for; I feel like I'm owed that much. I gaze at the cover. The wind shifts direction and flips it open. And then page after page turn, as if an invisible hand is at work. I'm able to read everything, and I'm able to understand.

Rebecca has created the perfect vaccine.

Not just for Covid, but for any disease where a virus continuously mutates, like HIV or the common cold. Using reverse transcriptase technology, she's developed a vaccine that can change itself once it is in the body to keep up with any virus by reengineering itself to match the new mutated versions. It's not the cure for Covid, it's even better. It's the absolute perfect protection against it. Against all the miserable symptoms sometimes even leading to death. Against the poorly understood long-haul symptoms. Against all of it. One vaccine for life – if people will take it. A way to fix the world.

I'm blown away. I knew Rebecca was brilliant, but I had no idea she was working at this level, way beyond my level of comprehension.

Rebecca is still standing, facing the sun. She's closed her eyes again and seems to be thinking. I'm worried for her now. Worried for the world. What if she falls? What if something happens to her? What if her findings are never read by anyone but me?

"Rebecca," I yell, "get away from the ledge. Climb down and go home now. The world needs you."

She can't hear me of course. No one can.

Her eyes open like she's had another epiphany, and she begins tearing up. "Dad! Your vision. Was it all true?"

She grabs her notebook and tucks it into the small of her back, secured by her belt. There's an urgency to her movements, and I'm guessing it isn't necessarily related to her scientific discovery. She needs to see her dad. She quickly climbs down the way she came up, and then disappears along the stone path. I realize I will never see her again.

For the first time since my death, I'm completely alone. There's no one but me.

All the pieces of the puzzle have fallen into place, and I'm at peace. My death has meaning. I've been a doctor most of my adult life, and I'd do almost anything to save my patients. My life for millions is a fair exchange.

I gaze up into the sky one last time.

As the falling sun pulls the last strands of light into darkness, I take a final glimpse of the living world and close my eyes for eternity.

Epilogue

A drop of rain falls from a distant black cloud high in the sky and hits Mark Spencer's sleepy forehead right between his brows. It trickles into one eye, waking him out of a comfortable stream-side slumber near Burnt Rock Pool. With both eyes now open and staring straight upwards, he spots the devious black cloud now hurriedly escaping to other parts of the world.

Just the one drop? Mark thinks to himself, wiping his eye with the back of his hand. *That's very stingy for a black cloud.*

He sits up, scratches his head, stretches his arms as far as they can go and then smacks a mosquito on his knee. He stares at the confluence of gurgling streams with their multiple eddies for a moment longer. He has a silly grin on his face, recalling the vivid dream he's just had.

I don't even have a brother. Nor a niece, for that matter.

This dream of death is *so* vivid, it reminds him of his old friend Rufus who died almost nine months earlier. Suddenly, not for the first time, Mark feels deep in his gut that something about Rufus' death in the warehouse fire *wasn't quite right* – a body burnt beyond recognition. Or, perhaps, *it was exactly right.*

My old friend ...

Mark stands and massages his cramped legs and then dons his backpack. He steps across the wide, beautiful stone embankment, careful not to slip, and then makes his way back onto the Towab Trail. His steps have a more hopeful spring to them. As he's walking, he thinks to himself, *that would make a cool story.*

He reaches into his backpack and pulls out his phone. He smiles, hits the voice recorder and, without missing a stride, begins, "I feel the bullet penetrate my skull, heavy with pressure, then darkness. It is the last thing I remember before I die."

The End

Author's Note

The challenge I put forth to myself when I began writing this novella was to begin and finish with the same sentence for no other reason that I thought it would be fun from a literary perspective.

While everything about the Agawa Pictographs is accurate, there is no "sitting stone." That was made up, so don't go falling down a cliff trying to find it.

The super vaccine that I describe, as discovered by Rebecca, is one hundred percent fictitious. Wouldn't it be nice though ...

In fact, you are allowed to hunt moose (and many other types of game) in Lake Superior Park *east* of the Trans-Canada Highway including along the hiking trails (like Towab), as long as it's the appropriate time of year. For plotting purposes, I had to take some creative liberties and say that it was not allowed. If ever you find yourself hiking that area during the hunting season, it would be wise to wear a reflective and colorful hunting vest, lest you walk in fictitious Mark Spencer's shoes.

I began writing this novella in August 2021, before I wrote and published the third book in the series, *Variant Reset*. It could have been the third book in the series but didn't seem to be going in that direction. I'm an avid solo hiker and do locum medical work (providing temporary services for a few days at a time) in Wawa – about 2 ½ hours north of Sault Ste. Marie – once per month. The drive to Wawa bordering the eastern edge of Lake Superior along the TransCanada Highway is world-class beautiful (depending on the weather!), as is the hiking in Lake Superior Park. Rugged and challenging, you can hike for hours, days, or weeks according to your needs, with great opportunities to focus inwards and discover all sorts of crazy ideas, like the plot for this book.

The vistas overlooking Lake Superior are unparalleled, particularly with the Fall colors. And there are historical sites, such as the Agawa Pictographs, that are gorgeous and educational. I wanted to incorporate all of these things into this novella while exploring issues surrounding death. The idea of incorporating the current Covid landscape came later, after I had completed the third book. Somewhere deep in this novella is an allegory to the worst endpoint of the Covid experience: death. No one thinks Covid will kill them anymore, and yet it still can. I think this is what was going through my mind when I began writing. No one in my life had died or was sick and approaching death, I was simply thinking about those people who caught Covid and, struggling for every last breath, unexpectedly died without ever being able to say goodbye to their loved ones, as if they'd taken a bullet to the head. From here I was reminded of the thought experiment mentioned in the opening pages: Imagine you are dead …

So, as morbid as it is, imagine you are dead … while you are still happily alive to do so, and make things right, if they need to be made right.

Book five will be called *A Covid Odyssey Legacy* and will be the last in the series. Look for it in 2024 or 2025, whenever this bloody Covid-19 pandemic finally and completely integrates and becomes a boring and unsensationalized part of our lives.

Acknowledgements

It really does take a team to make a book shine. Those missing words, doubled words, extra words. Those homophones and compound adjectives. Those nasty, nasty commas. British versus American spelling. When to capitalize, and when not to. The sentences that seem to make perfect sense in your head and even on the page, until you have a beta reader point out that it's really gobbledygook. The elegant plot lines that evaporate under closer scrutiny.

And so, it is with great admiration and thankfulness that I acknowledge the members of my team.

First wave readers

Andrea Reibmayr, always the first to read. She who measures the value of a story by how many times she cries (four times for this novella!) or laughs.

Dr. Laura Cody, my writing partner who seems to love editing almost as much as writing. Thank goodness!

Calt (N) (ret'd) Kim Kubeck, my cousin and oldest friend whose uncanny eye for detail makes everything that much better. Also, Rufus's biggest fan ☺

Dr. Brynlea Barbeau, a voracious reader who sits on my left shoulder at all times counseling me (in my head and by email) on the appropriate treatment (from a writing perspective) of those afflicted with drug and alcohol addictions.

Amy Wheeler Reich, who's attention to detail brings out the best in my writing.

Dr. Mike Cotterill and Dr. Anj Oberai, newest members of the team and husband/wife anchor of the Wawa Family Health Team in Wawa. For this novella, they were my "attention to detail" that only locals could know.

Cynthia Clement, my go to person for all things related to the publishing industry.

Chris Belsito, my go to person for all things related to public relations.

Second wave readers

Once all the kinks are ironed out, you need readers that can see the big picture and provide the necessary feedback. Monumental thank yous to: *Andrea Wacker, Dr. Robin Lewis-Palmer, Kelly McDavid,* and *Patricia Gelmych.*

Finally, none of this would be possible without the exceptional childhood provided by my parents, *Connie and Murray Elder*. Love you both dearly.

About the Author

Dr. Graham Elder was born in Montreal and attended McGill University for thirteen years, completing degrees in Physiotherapy, Medicine, and Orthopaedic Surgery. He now lives with his wife and two children (when they are not at university) in the small town of Sault Ste. Marie in Northern Ontario, cresting the shorelines of beautiful Lake Superior, where he runs a busy surgical and academic practice with writing time divided between scientific publications and novels.

Learn more about the author at:

https://www.twodocswriting.com
https://www.grahamelder.com

About the Author

BOOKS IN THIS SERIES

A COVID ODYSSEY

Snapshots in time of the Covid-19 pandemic as told through the escapism adventures of ER physician, Dr. Mark Spencer.

Amazon bestselling series featured as part of the Pandemic Collection in the Museum of Health Care at Kingston.

Written during the pandemic, about the pandemic.

Book 1 - A Covid Odyssey

A race against time to bring the cure for a deadly virus to a dying spouse.

Although the COVID-19 pandemic is ravaging the world, Dr. Mark Spencer's small town in Northern Ontario is largely unaffected other than being in lockdown and preparing for the potential onslaught. When his wife, Sarah – already attending a conference in Florida when the borders close – becomes deathly ill, she is admitted to a local hospital with minimal resources to treat Covid patients. As she spirals downward and with time running out, Mark concocts a plan to bring her an experimental anti-viral drug that might save her life. He must first, however, cross the Ontario/Michigan border and then travel 2000 km through a pandemic American landscape. Along his journey, he encounters a variety of unusual characters that bring into question the very foundation of his scientific beliefs.

Will Mark arrive at the hospital in time to save his wife?

No matter what, Mark's life will be forever changed by his Covid Odyssey.

Book 2 - Second Wave

A physician's harrowing intercontinental journey to uncover a dying father's potential cure for Covid-19.

Dr. Mark Spencer's life has finally returned to some degree of pandemic normalcy when he receives a heart-breaking phone call from his mother, who lives in England. His estranged father, a well-known virologist, has Covid and is being admitted to hospital.

That same day, a letter arrives in the mailbox claiming that his father has discovered a cure for Covid-19, but that, for reasons unclear, Mark must go to England to retrieve it.

Deciding that the possibility of a cure outweighs all else, Mark embarks on a gut-wrenching transatlantic trek that will ultimately push his resilience to the very limit.

Will Mark's treacherous voyage deliver him in time to uncover his father's secrets?

Join Dr. Spencer as he once again tackles the pandemic landscape in A Covid Odyssey – Second Wave.

Book 3 - Variant Reset

How far would a father go to save his dying daughter?

Alpha, Beta, Gamma, Delta . . . Omicron . . . Greek letters that have plummeted our world into chaos and tragedy.

Dr. Mark and Sarah Spencer are the proud parents of baby June, now four months old, born during the pandemic. The deadly Delta wave is waning, but there is a new variant on the horizon, the ferociously contagious Omicron that has a mortal predilection for infants. Somehow, despite every conceivable precaution, June has it and is quickly spiralling downhill.

Thanks to his father's research, Mark has spent the last year developing a drug that could cure not only Covid but all viral diseases, potentially changing a world on the verge of lockdown implosion. His team is close, so close, however, the well of their special ingredient has run dry, thanks to supply chain disruption. But an alternate source has been found in Central America at a location known only by one man.

Mark embarks on a transcontinental journey to beat the clock and save his daughter. There's a catch: A billion-dollar industry, Big Pharma, that wants to stop him.

Using every conceivable manner of transportation, Mark and his two friends will risk everything to save his daughter.

Wouldn't you?

Join Dr. Spencer as he struggles through the pandemic landscape for a third time in A Covid Odyssey – Variant Reset.

Book 4 - End In Sight

Death is not always the end ...

While hiking the deep woods of Lake Superior Park in Northern Ontario, an innocent man is shot and killed. Somehow straddling the world of the living and the dead, he realizes he has until sunset to make peace with the loss of his loved ones and make sense of the reasons behind his death.

A reluctant killer.
A small-town deputy chief on the hunt for a murderer.
A wife who would do anything to protect her husband.
A niece on the verge of a monumental scientific discovery.
A physician on a mercy mission.

Five individuals whose paths cross over the course of a single day, changing their lives forever.

Follow Dr. Mark Spencer on a magical journey between worlds as he unravels the mystery and discovers something that could change the course of the pandemic.

www.ingramcontent.com/pod-product-compliance
Lightning Source LLC
Chambersburg PA
CBHW031004210726
48290CB00007B/2459